Pierce

Pierce

Patrick B. Simpson

Apprentice
House Press
Loyola University Maryland

First Edition

Hardcover ISBN: 978-1-62720-493-4
Paperback ISBN: 978-1-494-1
Ebook ISBN: 978-1-62720-495-8

Cover by Katie McDonnell
Internal Design by Apprentice House Press
Editorial Development by Jack Stromberg & Carlos Balazs

Photo by Rubén Rodriguez on Unsplash

Published by Apprentice House Press

Apprentice
House Press
Loyola University Maryland

Loyola University Maryland
4501 N. Charles Street, Baltimore, MD 21210
410.617.5265
www.ApprenticeHouse.com
info@ApprenticeHouse.com

To Melanie,

For your teachings and support throughout my journey.

1

I only had a few minutes to study the crime scene before alerting the authorities.

Danielle Hutchins' body was facedown, blood surrounding the top half of the corpse. The dying sun of the day shone its rays through the opened window blinds, making a spotlight on the victim. I turned her body over. Her natural blonde hair turned into a cartoonish orange from the blood. Her lifeless blue eyes were open, but no movement from her body. She still wore the same dark skirt and light blue shirt I had seen her wearing hours earlier. It was difficult to check her pulse from the blood covering her throat. Once I did, I knew there wasn't any life left in her. A hole with blood oozing out looked to be around the size of a pencil. I looked around for any weapon but came up empty.

I crouched next to the body, putting my hands together to make one fist and putting it under my chin. As I observed the crime scene, unable to take my eyes away from it, I was taken back through the past couple of days with Danielle.

A day prior, washing my hands after I had gotten done cleaning the men's bathroom in the English Department, I went into the faculty bathroom for lunch. The room was empty, giving me the calm I was looking for while eating a roast beef sandwich. I sat in a metal chair at one of the white, circular tables. Ten minutes went by uninterrupted before Danielle entered the room. She wore jeans and a dark, plain T-shirt. She brown bagged her lunch. When she spotted me, she gave me a smile that made me forget everything.

"Excuse me," she said, lightly touching the chair opposite me, "do you mind if I sit with you?"

"No one else is using it."

"I've got a few minutes before I have to get back."

After sitting down, she took out a roast beef sandwich wrapped in cellophane. She caught sight of me taking a bite into my sandwich. We both laughed. The best icebreaker without saying much.

The few minutes were spent with the usual small talk one coworker would make with the other. She made a joke about how she was amazed most of her students were able to make it to community college. I told her I felt the same. Before she walked out, she asked me if I wanted to get a drink together after work. I quickly said yes.

Hours later we met for happy hour at Fitzgerald's piano bar in the downtown area. It was a place the professors and instructors normally went after work. The atmosphere was calm, and the vintage jazz interior made me feel at peace. We took a small table towards the back so we could talk and listen to music at the same time.

We took the time to have a conversation that didn't end with her running back to her students, nor me to my mop and broom. It felt good to sit across a table with someone who didn't judge me and actually wanted to speak with someone lower on the social ladder. At times, from the corner of my eye, I could see other people looking at me like I didn't belong. Whatever ignorance they wanted me to feel didn't compare to Danielle's charm.

I don't have time to go through every minute of our date, but when you are staring at the dead body of someone who was laughing at your corny jokes the day before, then you want to high-light things that might've seemed suspicious. One of those was her part time job at Brewer's Bar. She half joked about how the piano bar was a nicer venue than what she was used to a few nights a week. "It's nicer to hear actual music than the drunks stumbling through Lynyrd Skynyrd before closing time." It was a job she didn't want, but ended up getting when it was one of the few night jobs she could get in the area.

Next up was her parents. I asked if they were still living in the area, but she told me, with a straight face, how they passed away five years previous. "They were people that I didn't always see eye to eye with, but we loved each other, nonetheless." I apologized, but she did her best to say how well she was doing now. This led into her mentioning Vince, her brother. She wanted to get away from her parents, blurting out random thoughts that popped in her head. This was another bad area because when she said her brother's name, a look of anger and distrust crossed her face. Vince was still alive, but her body language said he was dead to her a long time ago.

I quickly changed subjects, bringing up how the pianist chose a tune from Miles Davis that doesn't get enough recognition. We spent the rest of our date getting back to small talk and making fun of the entitled students. Besides talking about her family, Danielle was in high spirits and didn't have anything that looked to bother her.

After the piano bar, I walked Danielle back to her car. We both asked at the same time if we wanted to get dinner tomorrow night. After a laugh, I said yes and she nodded. I told her I would pick her up from her class tomorrow after she was done. As I watched Danielle drive off, I felt like things were finally going to look up for me.

The only time the next day I saw Danielle was passing her classroom while she was teaching. It was only for a few seconds, but there was nothing about her that seemed frightened for her life. She was giving a lecture; everything seemed to be normal. I didn't see her for lunch because of the backlog of work that needed to be done.

I snapped out of my train of thought and returned to the crime scene. I didn't want to waste time thinking about details I could go over later. I had to put my mind in the now.

There weren't any signs from the killer. I didn't see bloody footprints, nor any bread crumbs I could use to point me in the right direction. At the same time, the place didn't look like it had been wiped down. There wasn't any strong smell of bleach or ammonia. Either this person knew how to kill or was the luckiest person alive.

It was recent, though. Her body was still warm, meaning the killer wasn't far. The problem was there are a number of places one could go to hide or find an exit before anyone realized what happened. The killer had to know the layout of the institution. I didn't see any point of running around the campus like a crazy person.

I looked around the room, searching for anything that might point me to the killer. Nothing looked to be taken, and nothing seemed to be out of place. Her classroom seemed to be in line, except for two desks at the front of the classroom pushed out of the way from Danielle's collapsed body. Even her brown purse was untouched as it sat on the instructor's wooden desk near the front corner of the room.

I didn't want to give anyone any ideas with me just standing near a dead body, so I turned to leave and find a phone. Before I got to the door, I looked back at her purse sitting on the desk. Sticking out of the outside pocket looked like a white business card. I gave myself another minute as I pinched the corner of the card, easing it out enough to see if there was any writing. It was blank. I turned over the snow white card, but found it to be mostly blank. On the top right- hand corner was a black cross. It didn't mean anything to me right then. I put the card in my right pants pocket to evaluate later.

Now, it was time for the authorities.

2

You would think a dead body in a small town would have the entire police force rushing to the crime scene, but they treated it like someone stole a few pieces of candy. When they did show, I took the rookie officers to Danielle's body. Both were dressed in uniforms that looked like they just picked them up on the way to their first crime scene. They acted like they weren't sure what to do, so they told me to wait in the main office until the detectives showed.

The main office was located towards the front of the building. No one was in the office, but someone left the light on. There was a wooden counter separating the waiting area from the desks and offices on the other side. I called out to double-check if anyone was still around at the late hour, but got nothing. I took the first chair to the right and sat there, keeping everything fresh in my mind.

I must've sat in the blue-cushioned chair for an hour until two detectives found me. I assumed they were detectives by the way their suits and ties were a size too big for them. They told me to sit still as they entered the office. The younger detective had short black hair, fair skin, and his shoulders were straight back like he was being judged. His partner was older and acted like he had seen too much. He had gray hair, saggy eyes, and a beer belly that had seen better times.

"Are you Truman Pierce?" asked the younger detective. "You're the one that discovered the body?"

I nodded.

"I'm Detective Longhorn," he motioned to the other man, "and this is my partner, Detective Johns. We need to ask you a few questions."

"Yeah, sure."

Longhorn's neutral face stayed the same. "We can question you another time if this is inconvenient."

Before I could say anything, the round cop spoke. "No, we need to question him now. We're not in the business of feelings and caring."

Neither Longhorn nor I responded. I even took my eyes off Johns because it felt like I was staring at the sun.

Longhorn searched his pockets as Johns looked me up and down. He licked his lips like a hungry dog would do with a dead carcass. He kept his focus on me like he wanted me to confess to Danielle's murder in the moment.

Longhorn flipped his notepad open. "You're the custodian, correct?"

"Yes, I'm the janitor." I called it for what it was.

"How old are you, Mr. Pierce?"

"I'm twenty-eight years old."

Johns gave a small chuckle, but I ignored him.

"And why were you in Ms. Hutchins' class this late in the day?" Longhorn asked.

"I was picking her up for a prearranged dinner we decided on last evening."

Johns snorted. "A beautiful woman like Hutchins with a guy like you?"

I kept my tone the same. "Yeah, not all people are shallow like you."

This stopped Johns on the spot. He took a step forward, but Longhorn put his arm out. I just sat there.

Remarks, like the one Johns gave me, were a great reminder why I didn't put a lot of trust in the men in blue. Plenty of times I was harassed by people whose itchy trigger fingers were covered in glaze. That wasn't the first time some know-it-all cop took one look at me and had it all figured out. It was more like a small dog barking at me and then running away when I stood up to him.

Longhorn continued. "And did you speak with Ms. Hutchins today?"

I shook my head. "I didn't. Last time I spoke to her was last evening."

"And where did you have dinner with her yesterday?"

I went to open my mouth, but my mind drew a blank. My brain could remember everything we talked about on our date, the location of the bar, and even what the slender pianist looked like. I had to give them something, so I just went what was on the top of my head.

"It was a piano bar in the downtown area. I, um, can't remember the name right now."

Johns snorted. "Already starting to switch your story, Pierce?"

"I believe you're talking about Fitzgerald's," said Longhorn.

It came back as fast as lightning, making me nod in agreement.

Johns raised his voice as he looked at his partner. "Oh my god! Why don't you just create this kid's alibi while you're at it?" He turned to me. "Stop with the excuses and wasting the taxpayers' time."

Before I could open my mouth and throw another remark at the assumptive detective, Longhorn told him to wait outside so he could finish questioning me. Johns huffed and puffed as he walked into the hallway, giving me the judgmental eye. This led Longhorn to roll his eyes like an annoyed wife.

"My partner has been with the business a little longer than he cares to admit." Longhorn brought his attention back to his notepad. "Anyways, where were you before you walked to Ms. Hutchins' classroom?"

"I was changing out of my work uniform in the janitor's locker room."

"And did you know anyone else that was still in the building besides Ms. Hutchins?"

"It isn't uncommon for people to stay late. There are students studying and teachers catching up on work." I lifted my hands a few inches. "Anybody could've been here."

Longhorn nodded. He wrote more notes than I thought he should be doing. Someone like Longhorn had the tendency to worry about missing a detail that might come back to bite him later. It was starting to become clear to me how high I was on his suspect list. He didn't look at me until his scribbling was satisfactory.

"Did she—"

Johns tapped on the window. We looked through the window as the paramedics pushed a black bag on a stretcher through the double-door exit. None of us spoke, only bowing our heads for a brief moment. Longhorn uncrossed his arms and put them down at his side, while Johns gave the sign of the cross. I lifted my eyes to see the doors close shut. Longhorn gave us a few seconds before continuing.

"Did she tell you any enemies she had or threats made against her?"

The only thing that popped into my head was when Danielle, accidentally, brought up her brother Vince. The look of unease on her face told me there was more to the story than awkward family reunions. At the same time, this wasn't enough to warrant Vince as a threat against Danielle.

I shook my head.

"And you didn't hear any noise from the time you changed to the time you discovered her body?"

"The area where I change is on the opposite side of the building. I didn't hear any signs of struggle at any point from changing to walking to her class."

From Longhorn scratching his head to Johns pacing back and forth, I knew these guys weren't going to find the killer anytime soon. I was already a step or two ahead of them. They seemed like a pair better for a buddy-cop movie than handling a murder case. I did my best to make sure my eyes wouldn't blink a lot and kept them focused.

"Is there any additional information you want to share with us?" Longhorn asked.

I thought about the card burning a hole in my pocket that I'd found in Danielle's purse. It was unusual but could turn out to be nothing. There was a quick second where I wanted to show him the unique card I dug up. He would take it, of course, but I could see them putting the cuffs on me for tampering with the crime scene. In the end, I told Longhorn there wasn't anything more.

"All right, Mr. Pierce," said Longhorn as he handed me his business card, "we'll probably be in touch with you soon. If you can think of anything more, let me know."

I made sure to put Longhorn's card in the opposite pocket from Danielle's. I didn't want to throw hers out from a careless mix-up. I gave Longhorn a smile like I would follow-up with him as soon as the lightbulb in my head went on.

Longhorn flipped his book closed, telling me to have a nice night. As he walked away, Johns took his time following Longhorn out. He kept an eye on me for a few seconds, a determined look running across his face. I could tell he already knew I was the killer before he actually had to do police work. He had seen similar cases in his long, tired life and didn't want to waste taxpayers' money going after phantoms when the likeliest suspect stood in front of him.

As the detectives hurried to their beds and called it a night, I had different plans.

3

After the show by the detectives, I decided to go to Danielle's part-time job at Brewer's Bar. I didn't want to go home. I wasn't tired, and going home just to cry over the past few hours wasn't an option. There wasn't much trust I had in law enforcement—my run-in earlier just another example of why. Any clues I could get right now would help me in discovering what happened.

I had never been to this particular bar, but it wasn't one I was eager to go to. The bar was located on the outskirts of town. A place like that was too evil for the churchgoers who balked at them. There were a few other stores on the same street as the bar, but people normally flocked to the brick building that sat directly in the middle to drink away their problems.

I parked across the street from the establishment. I figured if a quick getaway was necessary, my Toyota Camry would be waiting. The look of the bar didn't scream dive nor rough house, but the moon hiding behind the clouds didn't give the light I needed to see it entirely. I looked around, seeing only a few cars. A weeknight wasn't street-filled with witnesses ready to talk to the cops.

When I got inside, it was pretty much the same number of people as there were cars outside. A couple sat in a booth in the back corner, and a guy with his back towards me sat in one of the high-top tables against the wall. There weren't any patrons at the bar. The bartender watched me as I made my way to the middle of the bar. It was the best place to get the drop before anyone struck.

"What can I get you?" asked the bartender.

His voice had a huskiness to it that suggested he had his fair share of yelling at people to get out. He was about the same height as me with dark hair and green eyes. His posture said he was ready to call it quits for the night.

I said, "Whatever bourbon you have."

He nodded.

He removed one of the glasses sitting on the shelves and then scooped up the first bottle of bourbon he could find. I waited the short time before asking him any questions. You learn a lot from someone by the way they move and interact.

"Danielle works here, right?" I asked as he put my drink in front of me. I had to be careful to use the present tense. Chances are he didn't know yet what had happened, giving me the edge before his mind went into lockdown mode.

He sniffed. "She does, but she's not working tonight." He turned his back to me as a way to say he wasn't interested in more questions.

I downed my drink. "Did you notice anyone harassing her lately?"

He put down the glasses he was cleaning and turned my way. Whatever niceties he had shown me went out the window. He placed his hands on the counter and gave me a stern look. "Are you a cop?"

"I'm not."

"Then what's with all the questions about Danielle?"

I had to be careful how I worded the next sentences. I didn't want to be responsible for starting a panic—even with the low number of people in the bar. I made sure my face was as cool as the drinks.

"Because she told me recently she believed someone had been stalking her, scaring her enough to stay home."

The bartender tilted his head without taking his eyes off me. "Bubba, break time is up." He nodded towards me. "Throw this guy out."

Bubba was exactly what you would think with a name like that. He was twice my size, bald, and with tattoos running up and down his arms. He wore a tight black shirt to make sure everyone knew he worked out. Bubba stood behind me. The tobacco breath lingering from his mouth was heavy on my neck and head. He lifted one of his paws and put it on my shoulder.

He said, "All right, time to go."

By this point, not only did I see Bubba from the corner of my eye, but the three other patrons with their phones out, waiting for a late-night video to post. I didn't let any of these factors deter me from getting to the answers I was hoping to find.

I kept my focus on the bartender. "How about you bring out someone in charge... or one with brains I can talk to."

The bartender smiled. "It's just me running this place tonight." He nodded towards the bouncer.

Bubba started to squeeze my shoulder. In one swoop, I was able to grab his arm by going under and to the side, twist it, put the left side of his face onto the counter, and then lift his arm up at a ninety-degree angle. My left hand kept the arm twisted, while the right put pressure on his shoulder. The bar attendees were out of their seats, a distance away from the ongoing action. Bubba tried to squirm a few times to release his grip, but every time he did, I put more pressure on his shoulder. The bartender's face went from relaxed to worried in seconds. He didn't make a move to intervene nor go for a phone.

"What do you know about Danielle that you aren't telling me?" I asked.

"If there was anything wrong in her life, she kept it to herself. Danielle was last here a few nights ago for another shift. She didn't give off any indication there was something wrong." He pointed to the door. "Now get out."

It wasn't the answer I was looking for, but I didn't have anything to call him out on. Slowly, I let go of Bubba's arm. I backed up while he kept facing the bar, rubbing his shoulder. I kept my senses heightened as I moved towards the door. The patrons were still standing, still with their phones out. I made sure to keep my face turned away in the dim lights so the cameras couldn't get a clear shot. All my senses told me the coast was clear to my car.

Before entering my car, I looked around to see if anyone was dumb enough to follow me.

I was a couple of miles down the road before giving myself the all-clear and unclenched my fists.

4

There wasn't anything more I could do for the night, so I went back to my place. I parked in the slim, concrete driveway, checking once again if anyone had tried to follow me. The 1960s era, one-story brick house with basement belonged to ninety-year-old Thelma Reilly. Her husband had passed away ten years previous, but she swore never to drop the last name. He had built the place with some friends, and Thelma had said to me a number of times she was going to die in the house. I rented out the basement apartment for half the rent she normally asked other tenants. The other half had me mowing grass, doing manual labor around the house, and any other household chores I could do without calling a professional.

I walked carefully around the house. I figured Thelma would've been asleep for hours by then, but I didn't want to make any loud noises to waken her. When I went through the walkout basement, I threw my keys on the circular, wooden kitchen table. I needed something to calm my nerves, so I went through the vinyl collection I kept in a metal box next to the record player. Duke Ellington seemed like the perfect choice after the events of the day. I took the record out of the crinkly sleeve gently and put it on the player. I made sure to keep the volume low.

I sat in one of the two mahogany chairs at the kitchen table, contemplating everything that had happened in the last few days. It was difficult to get a good read on someone you didn't know well. Originally, I had thought Danielle had a lot on her mind and wanted to get dinner with someone to blow off a little steam. I wasn't anywhere near the she's-running-from-something ballpark.

Had someone set her up? Could someone close to her go the distance of betraying her to the point of murder?

There were too many possibilities to consider, but I couldn't just waste my time putting together a thousand-piece puzzle with only a dozen pieces. I thought going to the bar might point me in the right direction, not a confrontation and fresh enemies.

I took the white card from my pocket. I studied the card like it was a book on economics and the test was tomorrow. I flipped it over multiple times, trying to see if anything else would pop up besides the cross in the corner. I even held the card up to the light to see if there was a hidden message. When I couldn't find anything, I stuck it to the refrigerator with a magnet like you would when your kid gives you a satisfactory math quiz.

I don't know how long I sat in the chair, my mind trying to solve a broken Rubik's cube. I didn't want to jump into bed yet, but my eyelids were making the decision for me. The sound of Duke's voice didn't make it easier. I started to close my eyes when the rotary phone resounded. I jumped and rushed to the phone that sat on a small table next to the stairs. I put the receiver to my chest, listening to see if Thelma was up. After a few seconds, I had the phone to my ear, asking who was calling. There wasn't any sound coming from the other end, but I knew there was nothing wrong with my phone. As I went to put the receiver back in the cradle, a voice spoke up loudly.

"Hello, yes, are you there?"

I put the receiver back to my ear. "Yeah, who is this?"

"Is this Truman Pierce?"

The male tone sounded alarmed, but maintained steadiness. The constant holdback of heavy breathing and stuttering told me this individual didn't go around making phone calls at midnight to strangers often.

"Who's asking?" I asked with a firm tone. I still had to be careful.

"Your number wasn't exactly easy to find." He cleared his throat. "Anyway, my name is David. I was at the same bar with you earlier as you spoke with the staff."

That was a nice way of putting it.

"The video I took barely has your face in it, but I had seen you on campus on my drive home. I have been going—"

"Get to the point or I'm hanging up."

"Why did you start the commotion at the bar?"

I took a deep breath. "First, I didn't start anything—just asking some questions. Second, why do you care?"

"Because people are speaking rumors of something happening at the college earlier—something about Ms. Hutchins."

"And who is saying that?"

"People on the internet."

I wanted to roll my eyes, but the rumors were accurate, for once. I guess my only astonished take was that they didn't know the murder took place seconds after it happened. I didn't see any way of trying to deny it. By the time I woke up tomorrow morning, everyone would know the story. I knew all too well my generation had the information out there before anyone could process the horror.

I said, "Ms. Hutchins is dead." My eyes closed with grief and my body became weak.

Even with the knowledge and facts he had already told me,

he remained silent for a few seconds. There's a difference between gossip and having the truth told to you. He cleared his throat a couple times before continuing.

"She's dead?" He said it more like a question, like she might be alive. "What happened?"

"She was found dead in her classroom. The police locked down the place and questioned anyone there at the time—including myself."

"And she was murdered, wasn't she?" He was breathing heavier now, more unrelaxed. "Someone wouldn't have made a scene like you did in the bar over an accident."

I started to grow impatient. "Do you plan on solving the case? Or are you just trying to find more nonsense to post all over the internet?"

"No. I called because I want to help you. I was one of many who respected Ms. Hutchins. If she has been murdered, then I don't want this to turn into the Cortz case from three years ago."

Linda Cortz had been murdered, but the case was still open. The cops hadn't done much to find any suspect in her death. All the police could gather was her occupation as a nurse and that she was found on the side of the road. I remembered all the pictures in the newspaper of Cortz and how the police, for a week, said they wouldn't sleep until the killer was found. After a month, Cortz's killer was in the rearview mirror and never caught.

David brought me back. "The way you handled yourself at the bar showed me you want to see actual justice done."

I sighed. "What I want is not to be bothered. Whatever you think you might know about me from a rectangular machine, well, you're wrong. I'm not proud of what I had to do tonight. Plus, the videos you and the couple shot tonight will have my face plastered all over the web."

"Nope."

"No?"

"The couple couldn't stop complaining how grainy the footage turned out and couldn't get a clear image of you—even in high definition. And, well, my video does have a better shot of you, but I already deleted it."

I wanted to tell David there wouldn't be any chance of working together, but in that moment a lightning bolt hit me. I thought of how things might pick up faster if someone like David helped me. I wasn't a hundred percent certain if he did delete his video of me, but he sounded convincing. Plus, who was I to give him a lecture about doing the right thing after what I did? I gave myself a few extra seconds to give him the idea I was putting a lot of thought into it.

"All right," I said, "I'll bite. We can meet tomorrow at the college."

"Great! We'll meet you in the library at ten."

"We?"

But he had already hung up.

I was ready to pass out. I laid in bed, first listening for any footsteps from Thelma, then spending the remaining few minutes on the potential meeting tomorrow. This David still had a ways to go to prove he didn't have any part in Danielle's death. I would listen to what he—and whomever he meant by "we"—had to say. There were clues I wasn't seeing, but David might, at least, point me in the right direction.

I let the calm darkness finally take me.

5

"I'm just too old at my age to be cleaning up blood. Truman, you're going to have to do it."

Mr. Henderson had been janitor for a number of businesses and schools for the seventy-six years he roamed the planet. He had given me this job when he realized he couldn't keep up with the fast-paced generations beneath him. A once independent, proud man, time had caught up with him. His gray hair and slumped shoulders weren't a match for his sharp tongue.

We both wore our matching gray uniforms. Henderson pulled me aside after I changed. I let him nervously tell me what happened the day before, explaining everything he heard from management. I figured he would want me back early this morning, so I had gotten up at the crack of dawn and showed up before Henderson. When I entered work, there were only a small number of people there. It was enough to hear people spread gossip amongst each other. I knew I had a job Henderson wouldn't touch.

"I'll take care of it," I told him.

Grabbing the mop and bucket, I pushed the yellow container on wheels back to Danielle's classroom. On the way there, I kept thinking how this didn't seem right. She must've been dead for a little over twelve hours now, but it felt like the crime scene had to be blocked off for weeks, for some reason. Besides asking

Henderson, I asked a number of administrators if I had to clean up the mess. Without hesitation—and with annoyance—they all told me the police had gotten everything they needed and didn't want the classroom to become a "tourist attraction" to everyone else.

The cops had already taken away the yellow tape, but a few students stood outside the door, looking through the small window into the room. I told them they had to leave, and they scattered with some reluctant sighs. I pushed the bucket into the room and closed the door. Everything I saw last night came back to me in a wave. Finding Danielle facedown, the blood, the body, the reality. I knew I didn't want to be in this room any longer than I had to, so I parked the yellow bucket next to the blood and started to clean. Every time an image of Danielle's lifeless body would pop into my head, I would scrub the floor faster, like cleaning the blood would take away the memory.

It took about thirty minutes to get all the blood away and then rearrange the classroom back to what it was. When I felt like I couldn't do it anymore, I put the bloody string mop into the dirty bucket and then started for the door. There was a face in the window, the same expression I had before I started cleaning. He had a brown mop of hair on top of his head. I had a feeling who this was, but I needed to hear his voice. I opened the door, keeping the stare on each other. He wore a Judas Priest shirt with jeans and green sneakers. He was a rebel in his own way. When I didn't say anything, he spoke up.

"I know I said ten, but I heard you were already here." David looked down at the dark red water in the bucket. "Whenever you're ready, you can meet us in the library."

I told him to give me twenty minutes.

After dumping the water and cleaning myself, I took a vacuum and told Henderson I would get some cleaning done in the library.

Henderson was half asleep at his work desk, not caring where I went.

The library was closer to the front entrance of the building. The size of the library was more than five times any classroom. The light blue walls and brown carpet hadn't changed much in the fifty years it had been around. When you first walked in, the wooden check-out desk sat to the right. The sixtyish Ms. Murphy sat behind the counter, giving me a small wave when she saw me. There were tables for students to study against the far wall, and rows of books to choose from in the center. In the back corner, away from most people, was the computer center. The school had put it in about fifteen years previously by throwing something together for the students after they complained the school should finally enter the twenty-first century. The computers were still the original, used ones the school purchased, and they didn't see why they needed them in the first place. I figured David would be there, so I pushed the vacuum in that direction.

David stood behind someone sitting at one of the computers when I rounded one of the library shelves. I didn't mean to sneak up behind them and spook them, but when I got within five feet, they both turned my way in unison. The mystery man sitting down spoke up first.

"This him?" the stranger asked David.

The second guy looked similar to David. He also had some-what long, shaggy, brown hair with brown eyes. He had on a Metallica T-shirt and wore glasses reflecting the light off the computer screen as he stared. If you told me they were brothers, I wouldn't have been surprised.

"Yes, it's him," I said before David could respond.

"Truman, this is Goliath," said David, motioning towards the smaller guy.

I said, "That's not funny."

"It's not supposed to be," said Goliath. "My parents are religious Christians, and they figured giving a strong Biblical name to a baby boy would be an advantage for me. God works in mysterious ways."

That was enough backstory for me. "All right, you guys got me here. What now?"

David took over. "We were up most of last night trying to find anyone that could be connected to Ms. Hutchins' death." From his dark green backpack, he took out a notebook and a number of papers. "We looked to see if she had any run-ins with the law or any connection who would want her dead."

David continued to explain a little further, but my sight was on Goliath. Normally a new face wouldn't bother me, but a dead body bringing us together wasn't your normal circumstance. He probably didn't notice, but I would occasionally take a look at him and got a feeling he was trying to get more of a read on me than I was on him. He would slow down his typing at times and tilt his head in my direction to hear if I would say anything useful. Goliath judged me more with his ears than his eyes.

"And you were able to pull up all that in one night?" I asked, pointing at the papers in his hand.

"These? No, most of this is for a class later, but some information I did find." He pulled out a couple of sheets from the notebook. "Ms. Hutchins had never been arrested before. We did find a report she filed against a student—Kevin Nealson. This happened about a year ago."

This conversation proved more useful than I had expected. I didn't know much about the students here, but Kevin was a standout. He played starting tight end for a university on its way to a national championship when Kevin was arrested for cocaine possession, leading him to be kicked out of college altogether. He was the type of person where going over a hundred in the fast lane with no seatbelt was the only way. There had to be some way for me to talk with Kevin and see if there was any relevance to Danielle's death. I admit, it didn't scream 'we found our man,' but it was better than constantly finding Danielle's squeaky-clean record.

"And why are you doing all this?" I asked.

This stopped David midsentence. Goliath did his usual: slightly turning his head and putting his ear to the conversation. David, perplexed, looked at me with his brown eyes. This wasn't the question he was ready to hear as he kept his mouth shut and studied my face. After a moment of thought, he gave his answer.

"Because she was the only teacher that gave a damn about people like me and Goliath."

Goliath was turned in his seat, giving me a look of approval and understanding. Looking at both of them made me wonder why I was doing this. Danielle wasn't just beautiful, but someone who made you feel special—even when the rest of the world stepped over you. I could tell Danielle would talk to these guys the same as she would anyone else—without judgment. I didn't need to follow up with another question.

"Anyway," David said, "it just so happens Kevin is having a party at his place tonight."

"And are you two going to the party and nicely asking Kevin if he murdered anyone recently?"

David and Goliath both looked at me as if I was serious.

Goliath said, "We figured you would have a better shot talking to Kevin."

That didn't come as a shock.

I said, "Ok, what's his address?"

"I can text you the number," said David.

"I don't carry a phone on me—they're more annoying than good."

Even Goliath, typing away on the desktop, turned his head simultaneously with David. Both looked at me with wide eyes and long expressions. I had seen these looks before and I wasn't in the mood to explain myself for the millionth time.

Goliath said, "But how—"

I lifted my hand for Goliath to stop. "Just find me anything useful about Kevin—or anything that can point us in the right direction." I almost started to talk about the card I found at the crime scene but stopped myself. "I'll be in touch with you guys soon."

Goliath nodded.

I looked at David. "Tell me Kevin's address and the computer in my head will remember."

6

Kevin's house is exactly where you would think an expelled football player lived whose parents had paid his way out of everything. The three-story, white stucco house sat on the beach, looking out over Lake Anne. Chances are you could hear the music, talking, and other noise pollution miles away. I had to park down the street a ways, navigating my way through the number of cars piled on the side. The lights radiating from the house seemed more like a beacon for lost sailors.

The air had cooled down after work. Before the party, I swung home to switch into a pair of jeans and a button-down green shirt. I wanted to distance myself from the janitor as long as I could without a nervous student asking me unnecessary questions. The temperature must've dropped ten degrees by the time I got to Kevin's place. It might've been cold, but what I needed to do and ask gave me enough heat.

It only took me a few seconds after entering the front door to know that I didn't want to be there. I recognized a number of students from campus, but there were also plenty of faceless people carrying on numbing conversations. I had to keep a low profile, but I didn't want to be that person at the party who looked like they didn't belong. I made a lap around the first floor, saying a few words to people but not getting roped into a conversation. I saw Kevin in the kitchen playing a sloppy game of beer pong. He had more beer on his white T-shirt than in his plastic red cup. The hootin' and hollerin' coming out of his mouth made me think he would be spending more time here than in other parts of the house. Maybe I could get a word with him when he tired himself out, but first, I needed something to make me think he actually wanted Danielle dead. I grabbed an unopened canned beer from a cardboard box sitting on the marble counter and continued my search.

I was about three quarters of the way through strolling around the first floor when I saw a wooden staircase snaking its way to the second floor. If Kevin wanted nobody to go upstairs, then he did a lousy job of communicating the message. There were a few people on the stairs, but the attention seemed to be staying on the main floor. I casually looked around before deciding it was all right to go for the stairs. I set my still unopened beer on a coffee table and made a break. I avoided putting my hand on the light brown rail, keeping closer to the inside.

The second floor's narrow hallway seemed to stretch forever. There were a number of white doors on each side with light blue walls covering the rest. I had to be careful I didn't walk into a room where someone could recognize me. I walked halfway down the hall, turning to my right and looking at a brass doorknob. I carefully turned the knob, peeking through to find an unoccupied bathroom. I shut the door and walked two more doors down, this time going on the opposite side of the hall. The same brass doorknob stared at me. I kept thinking I would find a couple having drunk sex when I opened the door. There wasn't anyone having sex, nor anyone in the room, so I quickly went in and shut the door.

There was no doubt it was Kevin's room. The walls were plastered with posters of either football players or naked women. His oak bureau was littered with liquor bottles, condom wrappers, and other items you would see an adult with the mindset of a fourteen year old have. The queen-size bed with Egyptian sheets sat in a corner by the window with vinyl blinds.

I had to focus and stop with the judgments before he brought another girl into his love nest.

I scanned the room, trying to find anything that would either point to him as chief suspect or cross him off the list. The closet was the first place to inspect. When I opened the door next to the bureau, I thought a number of items would fall on me considering how full the space was. After a minute of pushing coats and shirts to the side, I didn't find one thing that helped my cause.

I checked under the bed, looked through the drawers of the bureau, and made a quick pass at the small table next to the bed. I almost gave up when, from the corner of my eye, I spotted a white object on the bureau. I had missed it before because a bottle of hair gel sat on top, blocking most of it. I would've dismissed it now if it wasn't for the tiny cross in the corner. It felt like I was smacked across the face when I pulled out the card. The completely blank white sides except for the similar cross I had seen once before. This was the second time in a few days I had discovered the same card. What did it mean? I pocketed the card.

After exiting the room and walking downstairs, I tried to find Kevin through the thick fog of people. My plan was to get him away from the crowd so I could get some much-needed information. With my head turned to the left, I started for the front door, hoping to find Kevin outside before he passed out. I bumped into what felt like a wall. When I turned my head straight, I stared at the same beer-stained white T-shirt I had seen shortly before. My eyes found Kevin in a surprised and arrogant state. It didn't take him more than a few seconds to realize my identity.

"Well," he said, "it looks like the janitor decided to crash my party."

When he said this, some of the crowd turned their attention in our direction. There were already hoots and hollers from the people telling Kevin to kick my ass. It became too hot for anything besides emotions and egos running high. I knew I didn't have a chance of asking any questions.

I said, "And the janitor is leaving now."

I tried to walk past him, but he put up a tan, muscled arm to stop me.

"Why are you going? Now we have someone who can clean up the mess." He poured his beer onto the carpeted floor. "Grab a big sponge and start cleaning."

I ducked under his arm and walked out onto the porch. My right foot touched the first of four steps when two hands pressed against my back and pushed me onto the front yard. That was it; no more walking away.

I stood, brushing off my jeans and shirt. I slowly turned and most of the crowd surrounded me and Kevin. The confident and judgmental eyes showed I didn't have anyone on my side at the moment. The one I paid attention to was the drunk jock with fiery eyes.

He said, "You show up, drink my alcohol, and now you want to leave?"

"I'm leaving unless you want me to knock out all your teeth."

The peanut gallery surrounding us made their comments.

Kevin's eyes widened. "You don't know who you're messin' with."

"I'm messing with someone who's going to wear the same work uniform as me in a few years."

Kevin's left fist hit me in the side of the head. The hit to the ground felt worse than the actual punch. The crowd cheered and laughed, telling Kevin what a badass he was. I didn't waste any time getting up like nothing had happened. The right side of my head was on fire.

"Is that what pussy ex-football players are throwing now?" I said, brushing my arms.

Kevin threw his right fist directly into my nose. This, once again, sent me to the ground. I felt liquid coming from my nose. Even with the large amount of blood coming out, by some luck, the thing wasn't broken. Kevin made the mistake of thinking the fight was over. He held his arms in the air like he was the second coming of *Rocky*. This gave me the perfect chance of sneaking up behind the gorilla without him hearing me.

"Hey, numb nuts," I said.

The second he turned, I punched him in the face. By the crack I heard, his nose was definitely broken. He covered his face, blood shooting out. Kevin knelt on the ground as he wept. He called for the crowd to kick my ass. Everyone turned; a few already started towards me. Before anyone could touch me, police sirens went off in the distance. All the rats in the crowd scattered on cue, leaving me with the ogre. Kevin still knelt on the ground when I put my foot into his shoulder, toppling him over. I took the card from my pocket and held it over his face.

"Where did you get this card?" I asked.

He couldn't stop squealing, so I asked the question again in a more assertive tone. Blood from my nose dripped onto his face.

"This guy... Ramone. I buy coke off him."

"How can I find this Ramone?"

His voice was weak, yet threatening. "He's the type that finds you."

I wanted to ask more questions, but the sirens were getting louder. I knew my time was done, so I hightailed it out of there.

7

I didn't waste any time calling David when I got home. Even holding my nose, I wanted to ask the guys over before anything else. David sounded like I woke him up but said he would be over immediately. I gave him the address and made a point of being quiet when the two walked around the house so they wouldn't disturb Thelma. When I got off the phone with him, I made time sticking paper towels up my nose.

I sat in my usual spot at the kitchen table, holding up my nose to slow the bleeding. Not only did I go over what I wanted to tell the guys, but also the fact that I'd made a number of enemies in a short time. Kevin would send any small-minded fan to come after me soon. I had to get my mind into the game because word was already spreading like wildfire.

I took out the card I still had in my pocket, holding it in the air to meet my eyes. I needed the bent card to be a reminder of my busted nose and the people I'd pissed off. My middle and index fingers held up the card towards the light to show me anything new I might've missed. I would occasionally glance at the card I had on the refrigerator door, and then compare the two. No doubt they were similar.

The guys had taken my advice with sincerity because I didn't hear a noise from them until three soft knocks on the basement door. Since I was already close enough, I told them to come in without having to shout. The tired looks on their faces turned off when they looked at my face. I told David to grab the wooden chair near the bookshelf and bring it to the table so the three of us could talk. Goliath laid the computer bag he had been carrying onto the table but didn't unzip the case or make any attempt to take it out. David brought the chair over and sat between me and Goliath.

David looked me up and down. "Are you ok?"

"Now I can see why you guys weren't itching to go to the party." I pointed to my nose. "You should see the other guy."

I passed David the card I took from Kevin's place. He picked it up and studied it the same way I had just a few minutes earlier.

"What's it supposed to be?" he asked.

"This is what I pulled out of Kevin's place before breaking his nose. I found a similar card in Danielle's purse when I found her." I motioned towards the refrigerator door. "The same texture with the cross in the corner. Does this mean anything to either of you?"

They both studied the card David held, and then turned their attention to the one on the fridge. David turned back to the card in his hand, staring at it long enough that I thought the paper would spontaneously combust. He shook his head in disappointment as he handed it over to his buddy. Goliath opened his mouth like he might've thought of something but shut it just as quickly. As Goliath pondered, David ended the silence.

"I have never seen the card before, but it is unique and can't be a coincidence."

I asked, "How about the name Ramone? Have you guys heard that name before?"

David said he hadn't, and Goliath, still holding the card, shook his head from side to side.

"I need you to look him up. It's the only name Kevin could

give me before the cops showed."

Goliath put the card on the table and took out his phone.

"I'll try doing a quick search," he said. "What's the Wi-Fi password here?"

I looked at him.

"Oh, that's right." He put his phone back in his pocket.

I said, "I need to get some sleep, but I need some information tomorrow. I might be a little late getting in, but I'll be there, regardless. We can meet in the library again."

They both agreed as they got up and moved to the door. David said he would look into the card, and Goliath was going to try to find any information on Ramone. When they left and I locked the door, I finally crashed on my bed. A raggedy mattress never felt so good. I didn't bother getting undressed or taking out the bloody paper towels I had up my nose.

The following morning I rose with a head that felt like an anvil. The blood had finally stopped, but getting the dried, bloody paper out of my nose felt like sandpaper. I only got a few hours of sleep, but it was enough energy to change my clothes and get ready for work. My nasal swelling had ballooned some, but I didn't have any trouble breathing out of it. While I looked at my appearance in the bathroom mirror, I knew I would have to make something up if anyone asked.

Drinking out of an expired orange juice container, I spotted the card on the table where Goliath had left it. I decided to pocket the card again, because either one of the guys might want another glimpse, or someone I hadn't thought of might give me another piece of the puzzle. I slipped the card into my pocket after washing my hands.

The first thing I laid eyes on when I opened the door for work was a beer gut. My eyes lifted to see Detective Johns giving me another of his smug looks. He got the bonus for coming over by the way he looked at my nose with enjoyment. There was ketchup on the corner of his mouth from whatever meal he devoured before attempting to ruin my morning. Detective Longhorn walked fast around the corner, telling Thelma they found me. Thelma started to ask what this was all about, but I shouted to her that everything was all right. By the time Longhorn caught up to me and Johns, Thelma had shut the door.

"Mr. Pierce, I was hoping we would have a word with you," said Longhorn.

"Now is not a good time. I'm heading off to work."

"Well, you're going to make the extra time," said Johns.

Longhorn sighed. "What my partner means is that we only need a few minutes."

Reluctantly, I stepped back from the door, lifting my arm as a signal for them to enter. Longhorn didn't waste any time sitting down at one of the kitchen chairs, while Johns looked around the apartment, quietly judging how I lived. He snorted when he saw the rotary phone. When he stopped judging and faced us, he gave me a look a teacher does with a C-minus student. I didn't bother to ask them if they wanted anything. I wanted them out as soon as possible.

I said, "I do have to get going. What can I help you with?"

Longhorn, with his legs crossed, seemed like he wasn't in a rush. "First, how did your nose end up like that?"

"I fell."

"Do you fall a lot?" asked Johns.

"You should wipe the ketchup from your mouth."

Johns' hand shot to his mouth and Longhorn rolled his eyes.

Longhorn said, "We heard someone matching your physical description was at Brewer's. The employees aren't pressing charges, but this can't be a coincidence. We're not hauling you in, but this is the only warning you're getting from us. We know that was the bar where Ms. Hutchins had worked. Don't think you're doing us any favors by butting into the investigation. Leave this to the professionals."

Johns put his hand down. His lips and skin surrounding were strawberry red.

There was no way around it, and I didn't bother coming up with a suitable lie. They were on my tail, and I had to be careful where I stuck my neck out next time. This wouldn't stop me from looking, though. And it only made me rise on the short suspect list they had.

"I have no problem putting the handcuffs on you myself," said Johns. He pointed to Longhorn. "You're lucky my partner didn't think we had enough to lock you up. Don't worry; I'll be there the next time you slip."

I said, "And how long did it take the two of you to figure out that was Danielle's second job? You've already wasted a lot of time, but it doesn't sound like either of you have come up with anything substantial. Have you arrested anyone yet? Have you stopped spinning in a circle since we last talked?"

Johns walked up to me, pointing a meaty index finger into my chest. The smell of hash browns and eggs hit my face like another punch. "What we do in our investigation has no concern with you. We're highly decorated officers, and I'm not going to be mouthed off by some janitor. I can't wait to see you behind bars."

Longhorn stood up, saying it was time to leave. I thought he would have to pull Johns away from me. Johns' face now matched his lips and skin. Longhorn put a hand onto his shoulder and pulled him to the door. Johns must've taken a number of mandated therapy classes in the past, because he took in a deep breath and then let the air out. They both took one look at me before walking out the door.

After closing the door, I watched their shadows in the windows as they passed. As much as I wanted to get to work, I needed a minute or two to make sure they actually left and not just waited to follow me.

In Johns' moment of anger, he did point out something I had only speculated on: I was their prime suspect in the investigation. It shouldn't have come as a surprise to me, but it did. I was not only on their radar but a target had been painted on my back. This was more of a reason to dig deep and figure out what was going on before I sat across the interrogation table with a man who wanted to pull the switch on me.

After a few minutes of not hearing anything, I walked outside to the car. When I opened the driver's side door, I turned my head to the left, then to the right. Neither side showed any sign they were around, but I still wasn't comfortable. They could've sat around a corner, waiting for me to leave, but I didn't have time for paranoia.

I jumped in the car and drove off.

8

I checked in with Henderson and a number of administrators when I first got into work. Each of them asked me—some with frightened looks—what had happened to my nose. I just told them I had a spill at my apartment last night and that it looked worse than it felt. The facial expressions from most of them told me they weren't convinced. Henderson told me bar fights weren't the way to go in life, and then he went into a rather long story of how he had gotten into one when he was my age.

After listening to another tale of the past, I started my workday with a casual walk around the college. I had plenty of time before meeting up with the guys in the library for our side project. I politely asked any professors or instructors I ran into if their classroom needed anything. Dr. Burns, the physics instructor, made a big deal about how the lights in his class weren't up to government standards. I eased his mind by reminding him Henderson had already contacted the electrician and that the lights would be fixed in the next few days. After Burns, I decided it was time to meet up with the guys.

When I got to the library, both David and Goliath were there, back in the same spots like they hadn't moved. This time no one was around, so I felt a little more relaxed than after good cop/bad cop had paid me a visit earlier. They each looked at me like they had found enough information since the previous night. This time, I took a seat next to Goliath, looking behind us to make sure we didn't have anyone snooping around.

"I'm guessing you guys found something noteworthy," I said.

Goliath took out a few pieces of paper from his backpack. "We did." He shuffled them until he found what he was looking for. "The name Ramone you provided isn't a common one around here, so the system only gave us a local arrest record on one person. He is a drug dealer who has been arrested a few times. Apparently, he is a middle man for a mysterious kingpin the cops have been trying to get for a couple of years now. Heroin and cocaine are the big ones, but he's also been connected to pills."

Goliath handed me a printout mugshot of Ramone before I could speak up. It was the picture of someone who accepted their life of crime. He had dark, short hair and skin that could be used as sandpaper. But it was his dark eyes that told me more than what David or Goliath could ever explain. I handed the mugshot back to Goliath.

"And why isn't he rotting in prison?" I asked.

"Because the D.A. hasn't been able to hit him hard with solid evidence. Witnesses at the time would go missing, evidence wouldn't stick, whatever. He has been more of a pawn with the cops to figure out the identity of the kingpin. One file I saw labeled the kingpin 'V.' Ramone is loyal and won't budge."

I took the white card out from my pocket. "What did you find out about the card?"

"Well," replied David, "it's used as a way to tell someone isn't a cop or snitch. They vet people, and then give them a card to show they can be trusted."

"Any information on Danielle being part of this group or buying them off?"

"None," said David. "We double-checked any crime reports linked to Ms. Hutchins, but the only thing that kept coming up for her was when she had trouble with Kevin."

What did Danielle get herself involved in? The only thing that she and that scumbag Kevin had in common was the one thing tearing apart this town. Did she get herself in so deep with these people that they killed her over the product? Did she steal for herself? Did she ultimately want me to protect her from people like Kevin because things were going south?

"How can I contact this Ramone?" I asked.

"You can't," said Goliath. "Maybe you can use that card to get in, but he seems like someone who beats the cops and the courts every time, and the fact that he works for a faceless leader will make it tougher than just walking up to him."

"Did you know the funeral was tomorrow?" asked David.

I shook my head. This was news to me. I hadn't had the chance to slow down and think of her actual funeral.

David continued, "The service is at a local cemetery, and then afterwards Danielle's brother, Vince, is hosting a reception at his place."

This brought me back to my first, and only, date with Danielle. Even bringing up her brother was enough to show her negative feelings towards Vince on her face and through her body language. All I had to go on was one person's feelings towards another.

"Have you guys met Vince?" I asked.

Both shook their heads.

I decided not to push any further. Talking to Vince as opposed to fanning the flames of opinions or rumors seemed more rational. My intention was to make sure the three of us were on the same page.

I said, "All right, we'll meet at the cemetery tomorrow. You guys can talk with any students that show up, and I'll work with the rest of the crowd. I want to see what I can find out from Vince. Maybe he can share something we're missing."

I thought I spotted one of the administrators walking by the window, so I told the guys I had to get back to work but that I would see them tomorrow.

After leaving the library, Henderson told me to grab the mop and bucket for a coffee spill in the hallway. I pushed the dirty yellow bucket about a hundred yards from the janitor's closet where the spill had occurred. I mirrored the back and forth of the mop to clean the spill with thoughts of Danielle going through my head. After several minutes of thinking and cleaning, I brought myself back to a floor that didn't have a speck of coffee on it anymore. I put the mop back in the bucket, and then started back to the janitor's closet.

I didn't get more than a few feet when I saw All-American Kevin stomping down the hall with three of his flunkies. The three minions wore the same brown-colored long-sleeve shirts and dark jeans. This must've been Kevin's idea of intimidating me. Kevin's nose was bandaged and looked a lot worse than mine. His red eyes were on a hunt, searching for payback. When all four approached me, the three dogs with him surrounded me. Kevin's smile said he had been planning this since the second I left him last night.

He said, "So, I was—"

"I'm not in the mood for any of your bullshit," I said.

"I don't care. You're going to pay for last night."

Jesus, I can't stand people who do nothing but talk. He still hadn't raised his fists, and the three with him were smiling at a joke they didn't get. I started to walk around him but he put his body in front of mine. Kevin took his eyes off me and put them on the lackey to his left.

Kevin said, "When I—"

I took the dirty, water-soaked mop and hit Kevin in the face with it, knocking him against the wall. Kevin's body quickly moved downward against the wall until his ass was on the ground. Water dripped down onto his shirt and across the floor. I hoped enough of the dirt got into his eyes.

Without thinking, I raised the mop horizontally across my body to defend myself against the stooges. My fighting stance looked like a wrestler—feet spread apart and hands nowhere near each other. Carrot-top to my right took a step forward, making me do a small swipe to get him to back up. My eyes went all over the place, making sure all four weren't going to do something.

"Hey!"

The voice came from behind us, but I kept my sights on the quartet. The three dogs moved their heads in the direction the voice came from, and ultimately decided it wasn't worth it. They helped Kevin get to his feet. Kevin meticulously wiped the dirty water off his face. The same look of defeat from last night crossed his face. He led the way back down the hall, and his three pals walked behind him, all with their heads down.

After the four went around the corner, I turned to see who stopped the confrontation. A brunette with slightly tanned skin and blue eyes that resembled Bermudian water had her arms crossed. She was around the same age as me, but had the older, angry mother look. Catherine's gaze at that moment suggested she was more upset than the people that attacked me. I took it as a sign that maybe I should leave, so I put the mop back in the bucket and started to walk.

"I need to speak to you," she said.

I rolled my eyes like a rebellious teenager as I dropped the mop against the wall so it wouldn't tip the bucket. Anyone walking through would see both items on full display and would treat the sight like a yellow cone. I held my shoulders back and head up when I approached Catherine. Her blue eyes seemed to get darker as I approached.

She said, "Two things: As an employee of this place, you should know better than striking any student. Something like this should be reported. And two," her face shifted from seriousness to a smirk, "I'm glad someone finally had the balls to hit that asshole. Step into my classroom."

Catherine was a lot like Danielle in the sense that I didn't know her well. A moment ago was the most she had ever talked to me. I knew she taught, business courses, but that was the same with every instructor I met in the institution. It wasn't because I was anti-social; it just felt like we weren't on the same level. It seemed faculty members were more interested in me cleaning a spill as opposed to getting to know me.

Catherine's classroom looked similar to the other rooms except for the business-themed environment. She had around thirty desks pointed towards the front where a whiteboard with the week's assignments were written. There was a wooden bookshelf around my height in the back, filled with different kinds of books related to the class. A small desk sat between the whiteboard and a window with a nice view of the forest's tree line. Catherine sat in her black leather chair a few feet from her desk. She didn't offer me a seat, so I just stood in place.

"How much of the confrontation did you see?" I asked. "Those animals were the ones that attacked me."

She held up a hand. "I'm not going to snitch on you, if that's what you're worried about. I did say I was happy someone finally gave a taste of that jock's medicine to him." She crossed her legs. "No, I pretty much saw the entire thing. People like Kevin think they are above this place when, in reality, they should be working their way up in fast food."

I smirked. "Nothing new to me. Listen, if you need any supplies or fixes around your room, let me know."

"I think I will take you up on that sometime." She folded her arms. "Where did you learn how to fight?"

"From my father. When he wasn't passed out from the bottle, he was teaching me how to defend myself."

"Is he still around?"

"Not sure. I haven't spoken to him in years. After my mother passed, his mental state deteriorated to the point where no one wanted to be around him. Right before I walked away for good he slugged me. I used the same moves he taught me to get away for good. We haven't spoken to each other since."

"I'm sorry to hear that."

Neither one of us spoke for a moment. I might've been blunt and straightforward with my answer, but that was always how it was when it came to my father. He was a hard-ass who taught me what I needed to make sure everyone knew not to mess with me. It was in that moment I realized that was the first time I had ever spoken openly about Dad. I was bewildered I had said that much to her.

Catherine didn't look like she felt awkward after what I said. She seemed to be analyzing me with her silence. Instead of going over my family situation in my head again, I used her silence to change subjects.

I said, "It seems like things have been going in a tailspin for the past few days."

This snapped Catherine out of her train of thought. Sure, it wasn't the most subtle way of bringing up Danielle, but it did the job.

"It has been," she said. "Danielle and I had been friends for the past year. She never once told me she was in danger of someone harming her. I just hope the killer is caught soon."

"Did Danielle say anything to you the last time you saw her?"

"Besides going on a second date with you?" She smiled. "No, she didn't come to me with a desperate plea to help her."

"What do you think happened to her?"

She lifted an eyebrow. "Are you an undercover cop?"

I couldn't tell if she was kidding or not, but she had a point, nonetheless. I was acting more like an impatient cop than a clear-minded truth seeker. I treated her question as kidding by mirroring her smile. I had to ease up a little and not push too much.

I said, "I just want to know, like everyone else, why someone would want to kill a teacher who was nice and didn't get into trouble? Does this mean other faculty members are in danger from this coward?"

"And I'm hoping they find the killer soon, too. There are rumors going around how she might've been involved with stuff no one knew about. She might look like an angel, but she could've been the world's best bluffer. But, like I said, I never saw nor thought about it when we talked to each other."

"Are you going to the funeral tomorrow?"

"Along with everyone else in this town. I'm guessing you will be there, too?"

I nodded. "I plan on going."

"I'll see you there."

I thanked her for stepping in earlier before I had to kick the shit out of those guys. She said she would find me when she needed work done on her classroom.

I found my mop and bucket untouched, and I pushed both back to the janitorial closet. I had to quickly put up a yellow cone where the floor was still damp before someone slipped and claimed the jackpot.

In the room the establishment calls the janitor's workstation, there are two small metal desks from the 1970s that touch each other, face-to-face. The room is slightly bigger than the janitor's closet with all the tools. When I walked in, Henderson was at his desk with his head tilted back, sleeping away. He was a deep sleeper, so my rickety, metal chair at my desk didn't wake him. I sat and thought about the new pieces had Catherine laid out. Compared to everything else I had seen lately, her answers were more in line with what everyone else was thinking.

Hours later, I wrapped up everything and punched out for the day. I stayed an hour after my shift ended to see if anyone would be dumb enough to try anything like Kevin had. After changing clothes, I was outside, not seeing a soul near my car. In fact, I didn't see anyone at all. My car was parked at the farthest end of the lot. I kept my senses aware as I walked up to the driver's side door. I fumbled through my pockets for the keys. I thought I lost them until I double-checked my right-hand jeans' pocket and found them.

I had just turned the key to unlock the car when I felt a presence behind me. I didn't hear anything, but I knew instinctively that there was someone standing behind me. When I turned, a man with dark hair, dark skin, and dark eyes stared at me. He wore a tan T-shirt and denim pants that looked new. It was like he stepped out of his mugshot. He was maybe a foot from me, but I could still feel his breath hitting my face. He didn't say anything. He only stood there, but I didn't need him to open his mouth for me to know who he was.

"Ramone?"

In one swift move, he punched me in the face. His fist half-hit me in the nose, the other half in the mouth. My back hit the car and smacked the ground. The last image I remembered was seeing

Ramone standing over me. He went back to his solid stance and didn't bother giving me a verbal threat.

My eyes closed and the darkness took over.

9

After I had finally come to, I found myself in the parking lot. I didn't know how long I had been out, but I did see my shirt sticky with blood. Blood was coming out of my nose again when I touched it. What worried me more was the blood coming out of my mouth. I thought I had lost a tooth, but luckily it was still there when I checked. There was a big gash on my bottom lip, coloring my teeth and lips in red. I lifted myself off the ground, seeing the key in the driver's side door hadn't been touched. I checked my wallet and pockets. Nothing was taken. Relieved, I got inside the car and drove home.

After walking into my apartment, I went past the record player and into the bathroom. The only strength I had left in me was to draw a bath and take off my clothes. I practically fell in, letting the warm water help me relax. I splashed water on my face, careful not to let my nose or mouth get irritated. After a few minutes, the water had a red tint. I sat in the tub for over an hour. Even when the water became room temperature, I still didn't want to get out. A few times I would put my head under water, trying to give myself any other feeling than pain. When I started to nod off, that was when I got out of the tub and went to bed.

That night I didn't dream nor have any nightmares. There were a couple times I woke up during the night from my nose hitting the pillow. And each time this happened to me, I kept my head straight and passed out within a few seconds. I didn't oversleep the next morning and I had decided to leave for the cemetery.

The next day I went to the cemetery for Danielle's funeral service. The sun was out in full force, but the temperature was cool. A large crowd had gathered to pay their respects to their favorite teacher. I could see people like David, Goliath, and Catherine gather with the rest of the crowd. I decided to hang back in the distance and watch the service take place. I made this choice because it gave me a great view of everyone who was coming in and going out. I wore a dark suit and a dark red tie—both I hadn't worn in years. I gently touched my nose and mouth, carefully not putting too much pressure on the bruises.

The service had just started. The minister wore all black. His mouth was moving, but I was too far away to hear anything. He moved his arms as much as his mouth. A number of people looked as if they were trying to keep it together. I could see Goliath, but David was hidden somewhere in the crowd. I hoped he was already asking questions to classmates and getting something noteworthy. Henderson had shown up, standing a few feet away from Catherine.

My guess was the gentleman sitting in the front by himself was Vince. He had few of Danielle's physical characteristics, but he made sure everyone knew they were siblings by the way people touched his shoulders and how they spoke to him. His skin was tanner than Danielle's, and his hair was dirty blond as opposed to Danielle's sunshine hair.

Somewhere in the middle of the service, Goliath spotted me in the distance. Thankfully this guy has brains, because he didn't wave his arms around nor make any sign to the others of my presence. The eye contact between us seemed like we were able to communicate with each other and understand what the other thought. Goliath then disappeared into the crowd for a minute, returning with David.

When the service ended, it seemed like everyone moved in a slow pace, as if they would miss Danielle's resurrection. Goliath started towards me, but David touched his shoulder and gave him a quick shake of the head. It might've been a few minutes, but the crowd, moving at a snail's pace, seemed like it took an hour to exit. When enough people had finally gone, the guys walked over to me. I got a better look at the dark suits and ties they wore. It looked as if we had coordinated our appearances.

"Jesus. Why does your face look more messed up every time I see you?" asked David with a look of disgust.

I said, "Were you able to talk with anyone before or during the service?"

"Not really," said Goliath. "We saw some people from our classes, but everyone was too sad in the moment. Trying to ask any questions related to her death wouldn't work."

"Maybe the gathering at Vince's place might help."

They both nodded.

Vince took his eyes off the casket and moved them around the cemetery. He didn't see the three of us talking or he wouldn't have felt confident enough to get up and slowly move away from the casket. He might've said everything he needed to before Danielle was lowered into the ground, but that didn't explain him walking in the opposite direction of the crowd.

"What do you know about Vince?" I asked.

David said, "Not much. Ms. Hutchins didn't talk about him with us. Do you want us to take a look at him?"

I nodded.

"Ok." David pulled a slip of paper from his pocket. "Here's the address to Vince's place."

I pocketed the paper. "All right. I'll meet you guys at the house soon."

Both walked away, leaving me with the ditch diggers and Vince.

Vince piqued my interest in the way he wouldn't stop walking in the opposite direction from the crowd. Most of the mourners had already escaped through the main exit. The more Vince walked through the cemetery, the less he looked over his shoulder. His walk was somewhere between casual and sprinting.

As I followed him, I kept to the treeline, acting like I was finding a dead relative. Vince made his way to a side exit that led to a sidewalk on one of the main drags. The ten-foot stone wall had a number of vines and roots growing from years of neglect. In the middle of the wall was a three-by-seven iron-gate exit. I didn't understand why Vince would go this way, but I would be exposed if I followed him out. I was contemplating my decision when a figure stood at the gate. The gate was open, but the figure treated the gate like it was closed. As Vince walked up, I finally caught sight of who was at the gate.

Ramone.

He didn't look like he was here to give Vince any condolences. Ramone wore the same jeans and shirt from the night before. His face looked like he was here for business.

Vince talked to Ramone for a few minutes. I was too far to hear anything, and Vince blocked Ramone so I couldn't read his lips. Whatever they were discussing it was worth enough to Vince to risk being out in the open with a known criminal.

When they were done, Vince shook his head and turned around. This made Ramone disappear around the corner just as fast as he appeared. I made sure to keep my backside to Vince, hoping he wouldn't get suspicious of the lone mourner in the cemetery.

He didn't once look at me.

The reception at his house was more important than anything else.

10

Vince's residence, a monstrosity, made me triple-check the piece of paper David had given to me. The stucco building had to be qualified, at least, as a McMansion. The white shutters, dark brown rooftop, and Venetian windows all had me question Vince and his family in a different way.

I parked down the road, taking in the surroundings. There were some people outside, but most of them, like me, were probably wondering where Danielle had come from. Henderson stood with a couple of the professors, waving to me as I walked into the palace.

If the foyer was anything like the rest of the house, then it was going to be difficult to maneuver through the crowd. From wall to wall were mourners, gossiping and telling stories about Danielle. A range of truth and rumors were bouncing off the crowd as I tried to walk through. I could hear them honoring her with stories that shone a light on her, but at the same time acting like detectives in a maze.

When I made it to the dining room, it had less people, but mourners were still bumping elbows. I had taken a look around for Vince, but it seemed I would have an easier job of finding a needle in a haystack. I also wanted to keep a low profile, but the number of people I kept running into suggested that wasn't going to happen.

A person I thought looked like Vince walked into the kitchen. When I started to get a better look, a hand delicately touched my shoulder. I turned to see Catherine looking at me. She wore a black dress that was a little too tight for a funeral.

"And here I thought you weren't actually going to show," she said.

"I said I would." I had to raise the volume of my voice a little to get above the crowd.

She examined my face when I looked at her. "You seem to be a popular person lately."

"Soon I'll be voted into office at the rate I'm going."

"I didn't see you at the cemetery."

"With the crowd, I'm not surprised. I was towards the back."

"You have that detective face on again."

"I do?"

She smiled. "A regular Sherlock Holmes, it looks like. I may not know you well, but I can tell there are other faces you can wear besides the one that is constantly thinking. I have been hearing rumors of someone making a ruckus around town lately." She eyed me up and down. "Are you the silent angel?"

"More like a demon." I did a quick look around the room. "I wouldn't be listening to unwarranted rumors and gossip."

"Danielle didn't tell me about the date between you two the night before she died."

This broke me out of the search for Vince. Catherine kept her focus on me while I put all of mine on her.

I said, "We had drinks at a piano bar in the downtown area. It was a nice time."

"'It was a nice time.' That's it?"

"I mean, it was only one date."

"What I'm asking is what did Danielle mean to you to make

you crawl out of the rock you normally hide under for all of this? You hardly knew her."

Catherine seemed to be pushing my buttons, for reasons I didn't know. She started to act as much of a sleuth as me. This didn't seem like a person who actually cared if two people on a date connected in a romantic way. I wanted to keep the emotions at bay, but I could feel the anger bubbling in me. Having to speak about Danielle on a deep level like this with a sea of mourners surrounding me wasn't exactly the perfect moment for me to treat Catherine like a therapist. I took in a breath and kept my cool.

"Because she was the only person who seemed to give a damn about me in the short time we had. Someone is dead and one of the last people to see her was me. Wouldn't you be out here if a guy was killed after going on one date with you?"

Catherine had on the same detective face as me. She was studying my facial expressions and body language, looking to find a place where the armor was weak. She turned her face neutral when she knew I was serious.

"Ok," she said.

Just then, I spotted Vince coming out of the kitchen and head into the dining room. For a guy who lost his sister, he looked to be the calmest person in the room. He was shaking hands and giving hugs, all while throwing a pearly white smile. When he went around a corner, I knew it my chance to converse with him. Once more, my attention shot to Catherine.

I said, "Sorry, but there's someone I need to talk with. I'll see you around."

She said goodbye as I pushed my way through the crowd. When I reached the dining area, Vince was by a bay window talking with two gentlemen in dark suits. A long table to Vince's left had been arranged with an assortment of vegetables, meats, breads and desserts. Most of the people had already filled their plates with free food, but there was still a long line waiting. I stepped in line because I didn't want to stand around. It wasn't long before the two men talking with Vince walked away. I only had a window of a few seconds before the next person would want to talk with him, so I quickly walked across the room. Before a heavyset woman in a too tight purple dress could say hi to Vince, I extended my hand to him. The woman, rolling her eyes, walked away.

I shook his hand. "I'm sorry for your loss. My name is Truman."

Vince took his hand back. "Thank you. It has been a difficult few days." He said while forcing a smile.

"Is it possible we can talk in private?"

He opened his arms in a semicircle. "As you can see I have a number of guests. Schedule an appointment with my assiss—"

I leaned into his ear and whispered that I knew about Ramone and what he had gotten himself into.

He held onto the smile on his face, but I could tell he was angry and astounded some stranger had sideswiped him at his sister's funeral. Vince took a few seconds to look at the crowd, then turned to me. His smile disappeared.

"All right," he said, "if that's how you want to do it. Follow me upstairs."

I stayed close behind him as he parted the sea. He thanked different people as he walked by them. I did my best to keep my head down and to move gently. At the bottom of the wooden stairs, Vince turned to make sure I was still there. He told a few people he would be right down and then started going up. At the top, the first thing I noticed was turquoise carpet matching the walls all the way down. The hallway seemed long, but we were at the door he wanted before I could take in all of the surroundings.

The room he chose was the billiards room. The green walls

went well with the pool table in the middle of the room. Up against the wall, next to the table, was a row of wooden cue sticks. The polished wooden floor had the same color as the frame of the pool table. On the far wall was a wet bar showing off all the expensive bourbon and whiskey. Vince pulled out two glasses from underneath the bar.

"What's your drink?" he asked.

"I wouldn't mind some bourbon."

Instead of asking what brand, he pulled out a bottle like a magician and set it next to the glasses. He took the cap off and filled a quarter of each glass. With vigor, Vince handed me one of the glasses. He stared at me, probably to see if I was going to ask if he put anything in my drink. Instead, I drank the glass in one gulp. Smiling, Vince did the same. We both held onto our glasses as he studied my appearance.

"What's your full name?" he asked.

"Truman Pierce."

"Well, Truman Pierce, you seem to know a lot about me. Are you expecting to blackmail me?"

I shook my head. "Not blackmail. I'm finding out what happened with Danielle. Since the day she died, I have been hit with more questions than answers. Her death has set off a chain reaction through this quiet town, and no one is talking. You, somehow, are connected with Danielle's death and I want to know how."

"And you believe this has something to do with Ramone?" He tapped his glass when he said the thug's name.

"It might have something to do with him or there might not be a connection. Every time a new piece of evidence comes up, he appears like a bad rash."

He took a moment to walk back and forth. The gears were starting to turn in his head, and I wanted to know what they were adding up to. There wasn't any denial Ramone had his grip around Vince's mind.

"You have more confidence than some cop," Vince said. He stopped his pacing. "How did you know my sister?"

"We worked together at the college." There wasn't any point filling in my job title.

He smiled. "Ah. Perfect Danielle teaching the next generation of consumers and greed. She thought she was above everyone the way she carried herself. Funny, how it all ends."

"It'll be funny when I catch the lowlife who thought they had a chance of getting away."

Vince lowered his smile, took the glass out of my hand, and set the two on top of the wet bar. He leaned against the bar when he faced me, studying me. I stood next to the pool table, not budging from my spot.

I continued, "So, what is it about Ramone that keeps popping up with your sister's death? How do you know him?"

Vince closed his eyes and took a breath like he was solving an algebra question. "He's my supplier. I meet up with him once in a while for my usual coke supply."

"And how does Danielle fit into all of this?"

Vince, once again, smiled. He pushed himself off of the wet bar and walked along the wall until he was in front of the cue sticks. I hadn't noticed before but each stick had its own design— its own identity. Vince meticulously studied each stick until he picked one out of the center. I wasn't sure if he was going to use it as a weapon, but I kept a neutral stance. The thought might've crossed his mind, but he backpedaled until he got the pool balls and rack from underneath the table. He laid all three items on top of the table.

"Danielle doesn't fit anywhere," he said. "I doubt that

short-tempered Ramone had anything to do with her, but I can't be so sure. Danielle, like I said, was little miss perfect to everyone. If you're telling me she was also in the drug business, then it's news to me."

"Where can I find Ramone?"

He laughed. "Beat me in this game and I'll tell you."

I didn't want to play any games, but I didn't have anywhere else to go for answers. I reluctantly nodded.

Vince racked the pool balls. He concentrated more than he should have, moving the pool balls until he was happy they were in the right spot. He took the rack away, setting it behind him on the wet bar. He told me since I was his guest, I should break first. This led me over to the wall where I grabbed the first pool stick I touched. I wasn't in the mood to waste any more time. I didn't bother looking at the design on the stick nor say anything to Vince. I bent over to line the white ball with the rest. I broke and ended up being stripes.

"I'll take it you and your sister didn't get along," I said. My next shot completely missed.

He kept his eyes on the table. "We didn't. Since we were kids we were always at odds with each other. I figured when we got older we would eventually stop arguing, but that never happened." He took a shot and made it. "She always seemed distant from me and my parents."

"Why didn't she like you guys?"

"She always wanted to be independent from the rest of us. Danielle made it clear since she was a teenager that she didn't want any favors or special treatment. Our father owned a number of hotels in the Midwest. He wanted to make sure me and my sister would be taken care of. Even when our parents were killed in a car accident five years ago, she still wouldn't take a cent."

"When did you talk to her last?"

"A few days before she died. It was the first time we had talked in months." He saw my mouth open for the follow-up question, but he answered. "She just wanted to see how I was doing. I thought it was strange since she hadn't asked me since we were kids, but I just went with it. She did say she was heading to work, but the phone call was at night." He shrugged. "She must've had a late class."

I replied, "She also had a part-time job bartending at Brewer's."

Vince missed his shot, the ball going completely wild. The look of lightning hitting his face told me he knew something. I tried to interpret the sudden change in expression, but he brushed it off like it was a fly. Annoyed, I returned to the game.

It was my turn and I was behind by three. All the geometry I slept through crept back. There was one stripe I pocketed right out of the gate. This was nice, but the others were on the opposite side of the table. There was a solid in the path for the stripe to sink in the corner pocket. I walked around the table, figuring out the best angle to hit the white ball. When I decided, I hit harder than I wanted, bouncing the white ball off the side and sinking the stripe. This gave me some relief as I easily shot the third stripe into the center pocket. The fourth stripe I took out in ease, leaving me with the eight ball.

During my comeback, Vince didn't say a word nor make any sound to distract me. I got the feeling he wanted me to win with the way he leaned against the wall. When he saw me about to sink the eight ball, he filled another glass of bourbon for himself and downed it.

I tapped the eight ball into the center pocket, spending a few seconds making sure the white ball wouldn't follow the eight. When the game was done, I laid the pool stick on top of the table, giving Vince a stare that said I wasn't in the mood for any more games—physical or mental.

I said, "All right, what aren't you telling me?"

It had been several seconds before Vince brought his eyes back to me. "I normally text Ramone through a number he gave me." He held up his hand. "No, he would know something is wrong if I just text him now. Ramone doesn't show his face often, and the number will go to a different person. He did tell me once, probably by accident, how he goes to Brewer's as an easy spot for him and his dealings."

And there was the piece he had been working on when I told him about Danielle's second job. His puzzled thinking was now mine, but I was connecting the dots better. There was a brief time I had thought she was connected with Ramone through her brother. Either Vince was a great actor or the wheels in his head were moving on maximum power.

"Did Ramone say what nights he visits Brewer's?" I asked.

He shook his head. "He didn't, but he made it sound as if it's a place he goes a few days a week."

I started for the door. "It would be better if you stayed around for a while. I might have more questions."

I wasn't sure if Vince heard me by the way he looked through the venetian blinds. He wasn't going to be bothered anytime soon, and I didn't need to be at the gathering any longer. I felt obligated to offer some condolences to him, but I left him there contemplating the new facts.

Our paths stretched further.

11

It had been three days since the funeral, and my only excitement had been staking out a bar for a potential suspect. For three straight nights, I sat in my car staking out Brewer's, waiting for Ramone to stick his head out. I decided parking down the street where I could still see who came out of the bar was my best option. On the third night, I sat in my car like the other nights, but instead of cold pizza to eat, I decided on a day-old burrito. There was a convenience store where I could use the bathroom—as long as I purchased something.

Every night, before each stakeout, I told David and Goliath where I would be. I wanted some witnesses to know my where-abouts, just in case I ended up the same way as Danielle. They were continuing the technical side of our investigation, but I could tell they were itching for more work besides sitting in a room with glowing screens. They might be pissed at me for making them wait, but I had a sense we were about to open an unknown box of hornets.

Multiple times, I went over what Vince had told me. It hadn't just been in his voice, but also in his body language. He first came off as pretentious and arrogant, but the layers slowly peeled away when information was swapped between us. You would've thought the man didn't give a second thought to his sister, but the facts I told him put his mind in a different perspective. I wasn't sure if I gave him more than a day's worth of thinking, but I hoped he took my warning of sticking around seriously. The last thing I needed was becoming a bounty hunter and running all over the country.

Brewer's was making its profits for the night based on the amount of people going in and out. Bubba was parked outside the main entrance, trying to act tough with each customer entering. The right side of his face had some bruising where I'd roughed him up last time. He was the only employee I had been able to witness during the stakeout. I figured everyone else must've parked out back, but there wasn't much room for me to scope them out without being caught.

It was a little after midnight when my eyelids started to tell me they'd had enough for today. Doubts were rolling through my head about the authenticity of the information Vince provided. I had decided earlier in the day that it would be my last stakeout night if Ramone didn't show. Valuable time was escaping from me as I sat in a parked car, watching as everyone moved forward with their lives.

I went to turn the key in the ignition when I saw Ramone walk around a corner and head towards Brewer's. My eyes opened like I was hit with an adrenaline shot. I hadn't seen him pull up, nor did I see him go or come out of anywhere besides that corner. Even with his back towards me, I slid down in the seat so he wouldn't see me. Bubba opened the door for Ramone like he was royalty, trying to give him a high five like they were old pals. Ramone didn't reciprocate.

When Ramone entered the bar, I got out, walked across the street, and down the sidewalk with my head down. I wanted to keep the bouncer unaware as long as I could before making it to the entrance. Bubba let in two brunettes when he caught sight of me. I wasn't more than twenty feet away. The red in his eyes and saliva dripping from his mouth showed he had been up every night imagining the encounter. He took a few steps toward me right as I was about to go through the door.

He said, "I was hoping you wo—"

I turned the fingers in my right hand into a C and threw them against his throat like Tetris. His knees hit the ground, taking in deep breaths to catch up. I didn't look back at him when I entered the bar.

In the bar, there were a lot more people than I had seen the first time. The age range ran from college to retired. The place was three-quarters full, giving me another cover from the staff. I didn't have a lot of time before the ogre caught his breath and stomped in, so I took a look around for Ramone. Time was ticking down and he wasn't anywhere in sight.

A spark brought me back as I spotted the same bartender I spoke with last time. He was speaking to a couple of the patrons at the end of the bar. His stance suggested he was ready to leave, and that's exactly what he did. He walked through a swinging gray door into the back. I didn't waste any time walking casually through the crowd like I belonged there until I reached the door. I checked to make sure no one was watching me before I went through.

On the other side was a long hallway. There were a number of doors on both sides going off in different directions. Each wooden, each with their own story to tell. It was a bit narrow, so I hoped no one would walk out and bump into me. As I walked down the hallway, I kept my senses on high alert from the anxious thought of someone jumping out and attacking me.

Halfway down, I looked through the small, oval window of a door. Peering in, I noticed a couple of cooks and other staff standing around conversing with one another. They didn't seem too concerned with the number of people out in the main area. My bartender friend wasn't in the crowd, but the staff seemed to be having their own meeting. I didn't want to be noticed, so I kept my legs moving.

The pull of my body led me to the door at the end of the hallway. It was the first one I'd noticed when I'd started down the hallway. I had a feeling some of my answers would be beyond this door, but I still needed to get mentally prepared. My hand sat on the doorknob for what felt like a minute. Numerous scenarios ran through my head for what might happen when I opened the door. I thought of how they could have their backs turned and be caught off guard. I thought they could be standing with guns drawn, waiting for me. Either way, I had to open Schrodinger's Box. I finally let my hand twist the knob and pushed through.

I took a step in and my gaze went straight to the poker table. Ramone, the bartender, and two people I didn't recognize were in the middle of a game. The bartender had the only look of shock running across his face. Ramone, sitting to his left, looked at me like he was expecting me to show. The two others turned to me with neutral faces.

The strangers looked to be working in the same drug operation as Ramone. They both wore black leather jackets, wore the same boots, and had their shoulders back like they were hired guns. This crew seemed to have a certain dress code they had to follow. The difference between them was that one was bald, the other blond. The bald one reached down to his waistband as if he was going to pull a gun.

"No need for that," said Ramone. It was strange to hear actual words coming out of his mouth. I thought when I finally interacted with him he would turn out to be a mute.

I said, "Careful with the hands."

Bald mirrored Blond, putting his hands on top of the table.

I took a few steps, stood behind Blond. I let the strangeness of the situation sink in for a few seconds. I would occasionally reach to my back like I had a weapon, but their faces looked like they were calling my bluff. Blond still had his cards up.

"A pair of sevens probably won't win you the game," I said.

Blond grunted and slightly tossed his cards on the table.

"You have to be stupid," said the bartender. "You're outnumbered."

"So why does it feel like I'm in charge of the room?" I asked. I took a few steps toward the table, watching their hands for any movements. "I'm here to have a much-needed chat with Ramone."

"Let me flush this piece of shit now," said Bald.

"We're treating him like he is untouchable," said Blond.

Ramone said, "Both of you aren't going to do anything, and that's the last time I'll say that."

Neither of the lapdogs said anything. I expected one would be foolish enough to say "but" and then have his head smashed in by Ramone, but they were well trained. Even the bartender had checked himself out of the conversation by folding his arms like a disgruntled kindergartner. Everyone in the room knew the conversation was between me and Ramone.

"So," said Ramone, "where do you want to talk? Or are you going to keep barking in here like you're a bulldog?"

"Let's talk in the alleyway." I looked at the other three. "Don't worry, your boss will be back soon to keep pushing you around."

Ramone got up from the table as I pointed to the door leading outside. He either knew what I was thinking or he was confident because he was walking out first. As he was doing this, I kept my sights on the three remaining at the table, making sure no one would be dumb enough to make a dash at me. When I closed the door, I kept my eyes on the metal for a few seconds.

The air was chillier and the nighttime presented a darker image than when I first walked into the bar. Maybe it was Ramone's presence that made the weather change before my eyes, but I wasn't going to act like I was cold for something I couldn't change. Luckily, the light from the street lamp illuminated the otherwise total blackout.

Ramone kept his back towards me for some time, pacing back and forth in the weak light. He wasn't pacing like he was thinking, but moving as if anticipating the next few moves. I could tell he didn't want to speak first, making me play a game of chicken with words. I stood in the middle of the alleyway. When he was ready to interact, he mirrored my stance; the light from the streetlamp showing the outline of his body.

He said, "So, you finally found me and put yourself in a shit situation. This better be worth it."

"How did you know I would be in the parking lot when you hit me?" It wasn't the first question I thought I'd ask, but it had been on my mind.

The whites of his teeth shone through the dark. "You really don't get it, do you? You think you know a lot, but you still haven't scratched the surface." He unfolded his arms. "You have one eye on us, but we have multiple on you."

I pointed to the door we had come out. "You mean you had your minions follow me when you got a whiff of what I was doing?"

"Any threat to us we don't ignore. The reason why it hasn't been broken up is we're always five steps ahead of everyone else."

"So you must know why I'm the fly in the ointment for you."

"I do. But I didn't kill Danielle, if that's what's running through your mind."

"Your name keeps popping up wherever I look, but that doesn't mean you're the killer. You're still high on my list, no matter how innocent you claim you are."

"We have—"

"I'm not interested in the power you have in this area. My focus is on Danielle, and taking down you or anyone in your operation that had any involvement. You punched me so hard I saw stars, but I'm still here. Danielle's murder is hanging over your head, and you want this solved just like anyone else. The longer this keeps going, the closer the law will be to your doorstep."

For once, Ramone didn't have any comeback. The nighttime might've shielded his face, but I could feel the conflict and debate running through him. I waited for him to counter my argument. He didn't take as much time as I thought he would when he finally spoke again.

"What do you know about us?" he asked.

"More than what someone should know after following the breadcrumbs for a short time. I know the drugs you've been importing into town have been numero uno to every person carrying a badge for over a year now."

I could hear the voices from David and Goliath running through my head as I spouted a number of facts they had given me. Whether or not all of them were true didn't worry me. I wanted to show Ramone how a janitor in his twenties was able to piece so much together in a short time. Here was my chance to show him I wasn't stumbling through the streets trying to find any random person I could pin the murder on.

I continued, "Danielle's murder is leaving open targets on everyone connected with the drug operation. I don't have any of the tools and gadgets cops might use, but that doesn't stop me from standing here and talking to you. I figure this murder is exactly what the cops need to finally put you and the guy in charge away for good."

"Are you asking me to help you find this killer that might or might not be working in my crew?"

"I'm asking you to take me to your boss so I can state my case before all of us are dragged off to prison."

Again, Ramone wrestled with the good idea I put into his head, but this time he didn't take long to respond. "Ok. I'll take you." He pointed to the end of the alley behind me. "My car is parked at the end."

"Right now?"

"I thought you were serious."

My stupid self was so shocked I was actually going to meet the faceless boss that I turned my back. Ramone did what he does best and snuck up behind me and hit me over the head with an unknown object. My lights went out before I hit the ground.

12

I didn't know how long I had been knocked out, but the bounce over a pothole or speed bump jolted me out of my forced sleep. I laid in the trunk of Ramone's car. I woke like I had drunk a bottle of bourbon the night before. I touched the side of my head, feeling wet blood. My arms and legs easily moved around because Ramone hadn't taken the time to tie me up. The last thing I needed was Ramone to stop the car and knock me out again if I started to kick the trunk open.

Being in a tight squeeze can slow down time to a snail's pace. If you're in a trunk, then chances are someone put you there. Normally, one would use that time to see what's in the trunk they could use against said kidnapper. Of course, Ramone wouldn't leave me with a gun or sharp objects to surprise him with when he would finally let me out. I didn't even have a tire iron.

What felt like hours came to a slow stop. The car shut off, and the only noise I could hear were the sounds of the night wind blowing. Ramone—or whomever was sitting in the driver's seat—didn't budge nor make any noise to signal they were coming for me.

The problem with this alone time is my mind started to come up with idiotic ways to make your situation worse. I ran through possible scenarios I could do to break free of my restraint. I thought the second my captor started to open the trunk, I would use my legs in a snapping kick to throw the door wide open and hopefully hit him in the face. Another scenario would've been pretending to be passed out when he came for me, only to fight my way out when he started to lift me out. The reality was I had to just go with whatever happened next because I was there to speak with the boss. Even if Ramone opened the trunk door and shot me that would've been the price to pay.

It was during this acceptance that one of the doors to the car opened, feet touching the ground, and then the door shutting closed. I used my eyes to follow the noise of the footsteps as they made their way back to the trunk. I made sure to keep my hands down on the carpeted mat so he didn't think I would hit him. My eyes were wide open when Ramone opened the trunk door. He seemed bewildered when we looked at each other.

"You really know how to take a hit," he said. His left hand was still holding onto the door just in case I started to attack.

I made no reply as he grabbed me by the arms, lifting me out and onto my feet.

"Run and I'll shoot." He took out a nine millimeter Beretta he kept in his back waistband.

When we started to walk, I finally looked where he took me. I had to give my eyes a couple of blinks because we were at an elementary school. The one-story, white brick facility sat off the main part of town, where the other schools were located. I was perplexed at first, but the facts I just stated made it seem like the perfect place for a meeting on drugs and murder.

Ramone had parked in the back parking lot, normally reserved for teachers and staff. The moonlight broadcasted over the paved parking area didn't show any other cars or vehicles, suggesting no faculty members were working late.

Keeping the same pace with him, I saw dried blood on the

handle of the Beretta. At least he didn't use it for its primary purpose. Ramone saw me looking and pointed the barrel at me, maintaining the same pace.

"Try it, and we'll see how tough you are," he said.

I smirked. "I'm realizing that was what you used to smash me over the head and drag me here. You could've just driven me here without injury because it's obvious where we are."

"It's simple: I don't like you."

We went through the blue metal door in the back, taking the first right. This led to a set of gray stairs heading to the basement. The basement itself led off to a hallway with a few doors, but Ramone pushed me through the room at the end with the double doors. It was a boiler more fit for the twentieth century. The old iron-style boiler sat against the wall, not making a sound. Luckily the thing was off.

A metal chair with handcuffs on the seat sat in the middle of the room. Ramone took the handcuffs off the chair and told me to sit. I did, and he wasted no time putting my arms behind my back and the cuffs on my wrists. He pressed tight on each handcuff as another way to enjoy hurting me.

Instead of giving me the next step of what was going to happen, he pushed through one of the double doors, leaving me once again with my thoughts and anticipation. I tried moving my wrists to see if I could ease the metal scratching my skin, but there was no use. My legs weren't chained to the chair, but there wasn't any point in walking blind all over an elementary school trying to find clues with my hands cuffed.

As I scratched my skin from the itching the bracelets were causing, I thought how David, Goliath, and Catherine would be able to find me if the night ended with me disappearing forever. I was being handcuffed, with no clue if my life was going to end abruptly, that made me finally start to think of how I needed to record my words and thought process to a video or piece of paper and then give it to my companions for safe keeping. I knew what I had to do tomorrow if I walked out alive.

There wasn't a clock in the room, but the time felt into the early hours before dawn. I stopped trying to guess when I heard tires squealing and music blasting from outside. Even under all the cinder blocks and bricks, the noise made me feel I was back in the parking lot. Discretion was of no concern to the person meeting with Ramone. It didn't take long for two voices that didn't belong to Ramone to come blaring into the building. It was Ramone who told them both to shut up.

I had expected the two mystery guests would come barging through the doors, cut me up into pieces, and then throw me into the ancient boiler, but nothing happened. I watched the door for several minutes, but it seemed everyone had forgotten me. That would've been my biggest break.

More time passed. I kept listening if the three were going to stroll through the doors or if anyone else would join the party. What scared me more than the two loud mouths was the silence that came after. I hoped someone would be stupid enough to just yell out that I was going to get a bullet rather than the constant whispering.

The door opened with a rough push. Bald and Blond from the poker game stepped through. Each had a smile running on their faces. I guess seeing someone who pissed you off not so long ago handcuffed with blood on the side of his head would make any-one giddy. They each folded their arms, standing side by side while examining the wounded animal.

"I didn't think it would be this quick to see the tables turned," said Blond.

"You really fucked up, Pierce," said Bald. It sounded like a slur when he said my name.

I kept my attention on both of them. They kept smiling as I spat at them. It didn't hit them, but both, after a few seconds, lost the smiles. I didn't realize it turned into a game to see who would blink first as we stared at each other. Ramone broke the game when he entered with a cushioned, brown leather chair with squeaky wheels on the bottom. He set the chair five feet in front of me.

"Is that seat for you?" I asked.

Ramone moved back and stood next to Bald. Just as I was about to ask the three what this was about, a woman with blonde hair, tanned skin, and a curvy figure glided through the doors. She looked to be around forty. She wore dark high heels to go with the dark tight dress that showed off her figure. This was the opposite of the overweight drug kingpin I thought would show. She sat opposite of me, crossing her legs and keeping her hands in her lap like she was applying for a secretarial position.

I said, "Are you mu—"

She raised a hand. "Don't speak unless I say."

"Are you going to scratch me?"

She kept her attention on me as she lifted her index finger and flicked it in my direction. Blond threw a fist across my face before I knew anything happened. Blood built up in my mouth, and I spat some to the right of me.

She said, "Now, any more questions, Mr. Pierce?"

I kept my focus on her with my chin up.

"Good." She brushed her hands. "You can call me Victoria. You have made my job a lot harder over the past week. Every time I find a hiccup in operations, your face is the first to show. The reason why you aren't dead right now is timing. The timing on the unsolved murder and the heat strung this along. A month ago you would've been hacked into pieces and at the bottom of the river. Behind me are three men that want nothing more than to take turns shooting you in the head." She leaned forward with her left hand under her chin. "Now, from what Ramone has told me, you are playing vigilante over your dead girlfriend. Is that right? You can speak." She leaned back in her chair.

I didn't waste the precious time. "The murderer is someone working for you. The coward that killed Danielle did so for reasons I can't think of now, but her death is connected somehow with your crew."

"And why would I believe someone working for me would kill her?"

"Because you said the cops are after you, and making one slip at this point will get you caught. The only thing incriminating I have found about Danielle is her connection to you. If I can find you, then the cops aren't far behind. Tell me what you know about Danielle and I can find the person responsible."

Victoria, once again, put her index finger up, but this time Ramone walked over. I was ready for another punch, but he bent down next to Victoria. She whispered in his ear, keeping both eyes on me. He shook his head a number of times, then stepped back to his original spot when she was done. Victoria, for the first time, smiled at me.

She said, "I'll tell you everything I know about her, but it's going to cost you."

"You're seriously trying to shake money out of me?"

Her smile widened. "No. I don't need to take the last two quarters off some janitor. What I want you to do is help out with some work in my operations since you did slow things down a bit."

I tried to hold the reluctance on my face. "I'm not going to kill anyone or do anything illegal."

"No, I didn't think a smart guy like yourself would go against morals and principles. All you're going to do is tag along on a couple of assignments with someone from my operation. Once you do these without any problems, then I'll tell you what her connection was."

When someone has you handcuffed and they give you a choice, this means you have one path to go down. I was stuck. My head would throb if I tried to process anything. I had become a pawn like Danielle, and I saw my life ending the same way as hers. I lowered my head to the ground in defeat while I talked to Victoria.

"How many?" I asked.

"Three."

"Are you going to give me a phone or something to track me?"

She shook her head. "Someone will pick you up and you'll join them until the errand run is done."

"What, have one of your minions follow me twenty-four seven until someone picks me up?"

"You might think you know how deep this goes, but you don't know everything." She motioned with her head behind her. "These three are only a piece of the puzzle. I have other people working for me. Cops, judges, and your regular Dick and Jane. There's a reason why I'm not getting fisted by a prisoner with bigger muscles than The Rock in a federal penitentiary right now. My spies are everywhere, and someone like you can't outrun the reach I have."

"When will my first errand run be?" I wanted to move the conversation so I could leave.

"Soon. Someone will get you—doesn't matter where or when—and you'll go with them. If you don't, the deal is over."

And with that, she got up from her seat and walked out of the room. The three behind her made a path for her to exit. Once she was out of the room, the others followed her, leaving me alone to think.

This was a shit deal. I was in over my head. I didn't have many options to go with, and Victoria made sure I was against the wall with no room to run. If she wanted me to give up, she was mistaken. I might've felt like things were out of control, but I wouldn't let her power grab faze me.

The point where she had me sweating internally was the number of people in her pocket. My mind went to everyone I had met so far and how they could have some involvement with her. I thought of David and how eager he was to work with me from the beginning. He might not look like Ramone or the other tough guys, but that might be the reason why I let him help me. I also thought of Catherine and how she seemed to be calm and cool with everything so far. She didn't look to be distraught over Danielle's death, but that didn't mean she was working for Victoria.

The real threat I saw were Longhorn, Johns, and every cop with a badge to kill. I had different reasons for distrusting law enforcement before, but now those fears were on a whole new level. Johns and Longhorn were the only two cops I had dealt with since Danielle's death. Where did their true loyalties lie?

Either way, I had to keep my senses on full gauge with every person helping me and potential ones that wanted to join.

Ramone came back into the room, alone, and took off the handcuffs. The red ring on each wrist burned as I massaged them. Before he could tell me what the obvious next step was, I got up and walked out of the room. I didn't sprint, nor give Ramone any excuse to take his gun out and shoot me in the back.

Out of the room, I didn't find anyone else. Victoria and the stooges were nowhere to be seen, and they did a good job of covering their tracks like they were never there.

Outside, I was still ahead of Ramone on the way to the car.

The air seemed warmer. I wasn't sure if that was because the sun would be up soon or I knew I wouldn't die right on the spot. There was silence between me and Ramone, but I used the activities of the night to keep my mind full.

I hadn't noticed Ramone's car before, but the black Dodge Charger blended beautifully with the night. Clearly, the man didn't mind showing off the rewards he purchased with blood money.

Before I could get to the passenger door, Ramone went ahead of me to the back of the car. He opened the trunk and gave me a cold stare.

"How about a ride up front for a change?" I asked.

He used his fingers on the trunk he held open to drum a wave.

I begrudgingly exhaled while I got in, nearly getting my head knocked when he slammed the trunk shut.

13

A few hours after Ramone left me back at my place, I sat in a local diner with David and Goliath. I could only get a few words into the rotary like "trunk" and "errands" for David to know we had to meet right away. I didn't get any sleep, and this showed when I stepped through the diner and both guys saw me—not to mention the new decorations on my face. The look on their eyes was enough for me to know they needed every detail that happened.

I chose the diner because it had enough people early in the morning where it wasn't crowded, nor would it leave the three of us as the only customers. The place had been built sometime in the sixties, eventually becoming a part of the town's history. It was the same size as a Waffle House and had a staff that didn't stick around more than a few months. There were four patrons when I walked in, all sitting on the other side of the room. This was good because I didn't want to whisper to the guys.

The guys had gotten a booth, sitting next to each other on one side. I was going to make the obvious joke, but my bruises wouldn't let me laugh. I took the seat opposite. They were here for some time from the two plates of eggs, bacon, and hash browns they ordered.

"Are you ok?" asked Goliath. He was trying to speak and chew at the same time.

"I'm alright."

Neither of them seemed convinced by my answer, but they just kept eating without being grossed out by my appearance.

A middle-aged waitress with brown hair and a smoker's voice asked me what I wanted. Her nametag said Darlene. She wasn't fazed by my appearance, scratching her head as she waited for a response from me. Even with the adventure I had just taken I wasn't hungry in the slightest. I told Darlene I'll just have a glass of orange juice. She made a disappointed noise in her throat as she walked away.

I looked at David. "Did you bring what I asked?"

He nodded as he chewed. From his pocket, he took out a video recorder and sat it on the table. The black and gray recorder was rectangular, with a lens in the upper left hand corner. It looked the same length as a pen. I had made sure to tell David earlier that I needed an actual video recorder, not his phone. I took the object from the table, giving an approving nod, and then handed it back to him.

Darlene came back with a small glass of orange juice. She sat the juice in front of me and then waddled away without asking if there was anything else she could get. Normally this would piss me off, but that was the farthest thing on my mind after the problems I had.

I took a sip of the orange juice. "When we're done eating, I'll need both of you to come out with me so you can record as I explain everything that happened to me last night."

"What did happen?" asked David, studying my face.

I started with my trip to Brewer's, and then told them about the elementary school. I gave them all the details but left out the part where Victoria told me about my ignorance to the number of people working for her. I was already choosing my words around them. There was still enough that happened to me overnight to have both guys unblinkingly stare with their jaws dropped. I thought they would have a number of questions for me the second I stopped talking, but they just pondered everything. Maybe this was the moment they would be scared and walk away.

I underestimated them.

"We'll see what we can find on this Victoria," said David. "Your description isn't anyone I know directly." He looked at Goliath, but the sidekick gave a shake of his head. "What do you make of the elementary school?"

"Not sure. I'll guess they don't use the same spot and move around constantly. That explains how the cops can't keep a good track on her or anyone else. Brewer's is a constant, but someone like Victoria won't go there, unlike Ramone."

"You should consider putting on a wire," said Goliath.

I shook my head. "Wearing a wire will get me killed."

"I could put a camera on you," said David, "but the camera I have is having problems."

"What do you mean?" I asked.

"I have a camera so small that most people wouldn't see it. It's the size of a Cheerio. You clip it on and it records a video to an app on your device. The problem is it keeps shorting out on me. One second it works, the next it goes out. I've been working on it for a month but haven't gotten it back to a hundred percent."

I wasn't completely onboard with that idea, but it was better than wearing a wire. I figured having a video of any illegal activity would be better than voices that could be scrambled or thrown out.

"Ok. See what you can do about the camera. Until then," I pointed to the video recorder, "we'll stick to what we have."

From the usual scraping of utensils and mouths chewing, the rest of breakfast was spent in silence. The guys kept eating their food until the plates were clean. While they were getting all the food groups in, I kept looking out the window. I had the sense I was being watched, but then chalked that up to the hysteria. I couldn't cut these guys loose, but there was a feeling someone from Victoria's crew was keeping watch on everyone I talked to. This was another reason why I had to move faster.

Outside, the sun broke away from the clouds, giving off a perfect spotlight for David to record me. Another reason why I chose this place was one side of the building didn't point to the road, giving us enough privacy to record. I thought of having them come to my place again, but I was worried someone from Victoria's crew would be watching my apartment.

I stood against the white siding, waiting for David to get the recorder out. Goliath stood to the side, occasionally looking over to see if the coast was clear.

I went over in my head again and again everything I wanted to say. The things I needed to say so someone who wasn't on Victoria's payroll could walk with the breadcrumbs I laid out. I especially wanted to make sure I didn't slip and say something I didn't want said in the moment. Keeping my emotions at a distance was key for me.

David pointed the camera at me. "Ok, you can start."

I opened my mouth and let the words flow out.

After breakfast—and my exclusive—I separated from the guys. David said he wanted to get home right away to upload onto his computer, where he proudly said it would be secured from any threats. Goliath didn't gloat, saying he had homework to do, but I could tell he wanted to think about everything I told them.

I drove back home to find Catherine and Thelma sitting on two wicker chairs on the front porch. They were gabbing away like old acquaintances. Catherine wore a white T-shirt and jeans—I had never seen her so casual before. Thelma wore dark pants and a sweater that looked like she had sewn it together. Her snow white hair she normally let go whenever I was around was tied in a ponytail, letting her ears get a breather for a change. It was amusing to see Thelma out of the house and laughing. Normally, she stayed in the house most of the day, leaving me with whatever chores needed to be done.

As I walked up to the porch, both shot glances at me at the same time. They looked like they were equally excited to see me.

"Truman," said Thelma, ecstatic. "I've been talking with your friend and she is a hoot!" The way she said friend sounded like a mother describing her son's girlfriend.

Catherine said, "Your grandmother—"

"Landlord," said Thelma with a smile.

"Your landlord has been great to talk to while we waited for you."

"Do I want to know what you ladies were talking about?"

They both just giggled, each pretending I didn't just ask that question.

"Truman," said Thelma, "I have not been seeing you around much lately. I hope it's because of this lovely lady."

I smiled. "Yes, I have been talking with Catherine quite a bit lately." I wasn't lying.

Thelma clapped her hands. "Oh, good. Did you know she's a teacher?"

"Yes, she told me she's a teacher at the local college."

Catherine was having a great time with this interaction. She smiled, trying her best to keep the laughter back. I looked at her a few times for help, but she wouldn't assist.

Thelma eased off the chair. "All right, I'm going in for a nap." She extended her hand and shook Catherine's. "It was very nice to meet you." Slowly, she turned to me. "Truman, before I forget, the kitchen sink pipe seems to be leaking again. Can you take a look at it?"

"Absolutely. I'll take a look at it soon. Just don't use it until I fix the problem."

When Thelma walked towards the door, she shuffled her feet. The first time I met her I thought she was going to fall down, until I realized that's how she walks. Even Catherine was ready to jump up and catch her. With the screen door closed, Thelma looked at both of us, giving a simple wave. When she closed the front door, I gave Catherine a quizzical look.

"So," I said, "how did you know where I lived?"

She went down a few steps. "It's not hard to ask around at work. You might come off as antisocial, but the other staff still talks."

I smirked. "Let's head down to my apartment."

When we entered through the walkout basement door, I offered Catherine a drink. She shook her head, saying she was ok. There wasn't much to the place, but that didn't stop her from looking around like I lived in a mansion. She took in the old-style kitchen and living room. Her eyebrows lifted when she saw the record player, and her eyes widened when the rotary phone came into her view. She spoke an hour's worth through body language.

I sat down at one of the kitchen chairs. "Would you like to sit—"

"I know you're the vigilante that's running around."

My eyes were on the other chair, and that's where they stayed when I gave a small laugh.

She continued. "There have been rumors of someone going above and beyond for Danielle. Your name came up a few times. And you going into P.I. mode the other day was a good confirmation."

I lifted my eyes to her face. "So, what do you want? To talk me out of it? To threaten you'll go to the police if I don't stop?"

"I want to help."

And there it was. It was the first question going through my head when I asked her the pointless others. Her curiosity was clear last time we talked, so it wasn't much of a surprise for her to be here. Even with the assumption she would ask me that question, I still wasn't one-hundred percent sure to let her know everything. Letting in David and Goliath felt like enough already, and the last thing I needed was half the town asking me to join some league. How many people did I need before enough was enough? Catherine could tell by my pensive face that she needed to sell me right away.

"The cops have questioned me and the rest of the faculty a couple of times already. They keep asking be the same benign questions, and it seems like they are stepping on their feet more than following simple leads. I sat for days, waiting for some small ray of hope, but I only got more rumors from people who didn't know any more than me. It's time to state what you did and find the killer."

"What have the cops asked you?"

"How did I know Danielle? When was the last time I saw her alive? Pretty much most of the questions you asked." She brushed her arm. "And you came to me first before any of the donut eaters did."

I uncrossed my arms. "And what do you think you can do that the cops haven't thought of yet?"

"They don't seem to know how to connect the dots even with everything in front of them. I can help you follow leads. You must have known something by now."

"I have found a few things I'm not sure if the police have picked up on yet."

"Like what?" She said that with a look on her face that was already connecting those dots. Some twitching and eye movements showed the gears turning in her head.

I gave her the details that would keep anyone up at night. I still didn't mention the two students helping me. I went into the meeting I had with the woman running the show. As I gave a description of Victoria, Catherine showed no familiarity with the kingpin's description. I then talked about the three tasks I was supposed to do for Victoria in order to get the necessary information about Danielle. Catherine did more mental sketching as I told her about my conversation with her.

"I can follow you for each task," she said.

My head shook. "If they see you at all, I won't be able to protect you. Plus, it doesn't sound like they will give me a heads up when it's time for each one."

When Catherine didn't say anything, I went into descriptions of Bald and Blond. I went into what they looked like, but didn't have any names for her to research. Even with the graphic details of the damage they had done to me, she still didn't make a grotesque face. She leaned forward with more intrigue.

"Maybe that's what I can do," she said.

"Do what?"

"I can follow one of those guys." She held her hand up before I could interject. "They already know what you look like, but they haven't seen me. I could follow them to get more information on what they do."

Without saying a word, I leaned my rearranged face in a few inches closer to her. I figured I needed to show her for the hundredth time why her idea wouldn't work. This still didn't make her budge.

She said, "With these descriptions you gave, I wouldn't have any problem blending in."

"And there's no way of convincing you to step away?"

She shook her head.

"At least keep me updated from time to time on what you do and where you go. There's no doubt they're keeping their guard up and being suspicious of every new face they see."

Without saying more, Catherine got up and said she was happy we were on the same page finally.

I stared at the door long after she walked out. I didn't like the idea of feeling responsible for other people now. Sure, they might've decided to be part of the Scooby Squad, but I was the one taking the hits. I figured each one of them would cave the second they were hit by anyone in Victoria's crew.

This wouldn't end well.

14

It didn't take long to be pushed along for the first task.

Before my two uninvited guests showed, I let my mind relax for once. I didn't want to think about the different scenarios this mouse would have to escape. A can of peaches was my only dinner that night. After taking the metal lid off, I sat with my feet up on the coffee table with the Duke playing the blues throughout the apartment. I didn't bother with a fork, using my fingers to take each peach out and eat it.

I had just closed my eyes when Ramone and Bald showed up at my door. This was a mental punch for me because I thought it would be days—maybe weeks—until I was summoned. When I opened the door, my face made it look like I was prepared to see them, but my mind sounded off the alarms. They stood in the doorway, not taking a step in—not like I would invite them, but they didn't seem the type to ask.

"It's time," Bald said, breaking the silence between the two.

Both men were dressed like they were going to a brawl. They wore dark pants and black leather jackets. The difference was Ramone wore a white T-shirt, while Bald went with dark blue. I wanted to point out it was a bit on the nose what they were going for, but I didn't want the fists to fly so soon.

"Let me grab my coat," I said.

Neither objected, but neither were they going to let me go anywhere alone. As I walked to the living room chair—that I also used as a coat rack—Bald stayed a few feet behind me. I was thankful I hadn't gone with the wire idea. He didn't say anything, but his presence in the room was more than any words that could be expressed. Taking my light jacket off the chair, I faced Bald as I put it on.

"Do you want to frisk me just in case?" I asked, putting my arms up.

He only grunted.

As we walked outside, Ramone stayed in front of me while Bald brought up the rear. The temperature had dropped to give me a chill. The moon gave off enough light to see whether or not one of them would pull a weapon on me. Not like I would actually get far, but at least I wouldn't look like a blind man.

About a hundred feet down the road, Ramone's Charger was parked. There wasn't anyone out, but that didn't stop Ramone from checking around to give himself peace of mind. When he was satisfied that the neighborhood didn't have any active snitches, he turned to me.

"You're going to be the driver," he said as he took a pair of keys from his jacket pocket and tossed them to me.

"And is this the part where you're going to tell me not to make a scratch?"

He didn't say anything as he got into the passenger seat, and Bald took his place in the backseat. Right behind me.

Inside the Charger, the leather seats were more comfortable than anything I owned. The dark blue glowing radio and sound system looked like it could take out all the windows up and down the street, but I didn't think I would ever find out. My hands gripped the steering wheel, the cushion relaxing my fingers.

"Where are we going?" I asked Ramone.

"I'll tell you when to turn and when to stop."

Even with both of them feeling confident I wasn't pulling any strings, he still didn't have me at one-hundred percent. There was no point in asking what would happen when we got to our destination. I always had a go-with-the-flow attitude, but this was different than letting some friends pick a movie to watch. The options weren't many, and I knew there wasn't a democratic process for what I was being a part of. I only hoped this night wouldn't end with me in a ditch.

I turned the car on and let the engine come alive. It wasn't loud enough to wake the neighbors. I wasn't stupid enough to step on the gas and let the car howl in the moonlight. My foot wasn't near the gas pedal as I peered over to Ramone for the first direction.

Ramone said, "Take this all the way to the end of the street and make a left."

Ten minutes later, we were still driving all over town. I felt there had to be a more direct route, but maybe this was some sort of way to make me forget where we were. Everything I had seen so far was nothing new to me. Being in this town for a few years had given me enough nights to check out the different parts it held. It might be easy for someone new to town to get lost, but someone who had been on those streets a number of times wouldn't have a problem.

Not many people were on the road at this time of night. By this point, Ramone had me going down backroads just to be sure no people or cameras would make the car out. I could've driven on the other side of the road for a few miles without coming across another vehicle. I had been one of those people only a short time ago. Closing my eyes at night, arrogantly thinking this type of crime happened in other places.

"Make a right."

Besides the directions, the silence in the car was a new level of discomfort. Both guys must've been used to being in quiet spots for long stretches. There were times I wanted to reach over and turn the radio on to classic jazz. I would take the Duke—or anyone—to keep me distracted.

"Take a right at the second intersection."

The problem with this type of silence for me is when unnecessary thoughts start popping in my head—much like being stuck in the trunk of the same automobile I was driving. It didn't get to the point I regretted everything I had been doing, but I obsessed over how I could screw things up if I didn't have my senses on high alert. Being a part of this sick game meant I could make things worse than they had already become. I didn't see any light at the end of the tunnel, nor think I would see any bright lights any time soon.

My mind turned to Danielle and wondered if this was the direction she wanted to go in. Dozens and dozens of times, I had already gone over the way she acted the last few times we spent together. Her face, her body language, and her tone were all things I had used as clues to help me with this puzzle. I had thought about it so much that, sometimes, I started to have doubts that her death even happened.

Was it worth it to be associated with any crimes that might occur tonight? I was out to find a killer, not to be part of something that could lead to more death and destruction. Finding a killer without turning into one seemed like a line that had become more blurry. This is where I had to turn my mind somewhere else and let the clues rest.

"We're here," said Ramone, pointing to an alley between an apartment building and pool hall. "Park in there."

The area we ended up in was on the outskirts of town. The

brick, five-story apartment building matched the area it occupied. The pool hall next door might've been nice once, but the owner let it slip with the rest of the area. There was trash on the sidewalks and graffiti on the sides of the buildings. The cracks and stains on both buildings showed why gangsters like Ramone and Bald flourished.

I took the car just slightly off the sidewalk. Before turning off the engine, I checked the green digital clock in the center console. The numbers told me it was eleven forty-seven as they disappeared. Ramone reached his hand over to me, palm facing up. Without having to hear the obvious order, I took the keys out of the ignition and placed them in his hand. He peered over his shoulder. I thought he was checking to see if the coast was clear, but he gave a small nod to Bald. Ramone opened the car door a foot so the alley would give him enough room to exit. I opened my door the same time Bald opened his.

"You're not going anywhere," said Bald.

Getting out, Bald walked over to the still-open passenger side door and took Ramone's spot. In the rearview mirror, I watched as Ramone walked around the corner and headed towards the direction of the apartment building.

"And what are we supposed to do now?" I asked Bald.

"Sit here and wait for Ramone to get back."

"And how—"

"He'll get back when he gets back."

We sat in silence for what felt like months. Bald would occasionally scratch his arm, speeding up time a little. When I would tap on the steering wheel or make noises with my mouth, Bald would threaten me more.

I wasn't sure if this was the beginning of my night or the end. It was a relief not following Ramone to wherever he had to go, but it didn't put my mind at ease when it came to playing chauffeur. Boredom started telling me to throw an elbow into Bald's face and then find out what Ramone was doing so I could use it later against him. I shook off the thought.

"My family owned a horse when I was a child," said Bald.

Bald's sudden statement stopped my train of thought. It took me a moment to register what he was saying. I thought he had given me my next set of instructions. When my mind identified the word "horse," then I was mentally back in the car. He kept going when he saw the look of confusion on my face.

"I grew up on a farm a few states over. There wasn't much to do besides work and stare at animals. My father would beat me any chance he saw fit, and my mother would've helped if she wasn't passed out from the bottle."

No point being a smartass and stopping him. He was on a roll, and I didn't see why arguing with him would make the situation better.

Bald kept his sight toward the mostly darkened alley. "My father had a horse he loved more than his own family. The horse had the type of white hair you would see in the movies. He didn't name the horse because he said a name would ruin the uniqueness of the animal. Whenever he would get done harvesting the crops or taking care of usual business, he made sure he had plenty of time to ride the horse for at least an hour a day."

"One day, my father took the horse out, but hours later the horse returned alone. Mom had already checked herself out with the whiskey for the day, so I spent over an hour finding him. I was ten. I found my father, alive, next to an oak tree. He was thrown off the horse and snapped his spine on one of the exposed roots. It took another hour for the paramedics to show up and send him to the hospital. He was paralyzed from the neck down."

Occasionally, I would catch him from the corner of my eye glancing at me. The more he told his story, the more he would see if my focus was still on him. My face might've been turned toward the driver's window, but it wasn't like leaning over and turning the radio off.

He continued, "For the first month, me and Mom were both helping the old man. Mom eventually decided it wasn't worth it, and then I became the only one responsible. I would get him changed, push him around in his wheelchair, bathe him, even wiped his ass. Even with me taking care of him, he still found ways to insult me. On top of that, the farm was falling apart. Every day I tried doing what a ten-year-old kid could do."

"Over the weeks my hatred for the white stallion grew more and more. When I had to go outside, I would always run into the beast. At first, the monster knew it must've done something wrong by the way the animal's head was down most of the time. I wasn't fooled. Every time I had to go into the stable to feed it, the animal would try to nudge my arm like he was apologizing. I would slap him away, telling him I wasn't interested in fake apologies."

"Everything finally came to a breaking point. Months later, after my mother left us for a better life in Las Vegas, I was in pieces and barely hanging on. One night I was helping my father out of the bathtub when I slipped, dropping him under the bath water. I stood there, watching the numerous air bubbles reaching the surface. Under the water, he stared at me with horrified eyes—the first time he ever looked at me like this. I understood in that moment how I had power over him. I pulled him out of the tub, thinking of bigger plans for him."

My head was angled to face both him and the alley. Someone like Bald didn't come across as a fiction storyteller, but I could tell he was putting a lot of emphasis on making sure I got the point. I didn't even notice if anyone had passed the car nor what my surroundings were like the past couple of minutes.

"I pushed my father, soaking, in his wheelchair to his room, where I dumped him on the bed. When I got him positioned with his back against the backboard, he shouted at me like he was a rabid dog. That was it for me. I walked over to his closet, where I took out a double-barrel shotgun he used to shoot geese. He screamed that I didn't have the balls to shoot him as I poured the box of shells onto the bed. I took two shells and loaded the gun. I then walked downstairs and out to the stable. I crashed through the stable door like a wolf, eyes for the one thing that I could blame. The horse had a face of calmness when we stared at each other. I took the shotgun and shot one barrel into the thing's leg. The animal shrieked and flopped on the ground. I stood there for a moment, watching as the beast begged me to end its life. I realized how easy this was, to take a life. When I decided what path I would head down, I shot the second barrel into the animal's face, finally ending the creature.

"I did the equivalent of dragging my feet back to the house. I knew the old man had heard both barrels go off. He might've been physically paralyzed, but that mind of his was still working. I reached his bedroom door and opened it slowly. I had made sure his head was propped up enough to see anyone that would come in. With the hall light shining, he could see my face covered in the blood of the only thing that made him smile. His face said pretty much everything I needed to know, but I still walked in and stood next to his bed. His eyes, unblinking, kept the focus on the blood. I flipped open the shotgun and let the two spent cartridges hit the floor. I took two more off the bed and loaded the gun. I pointed the weapon at his face, telling him things were going to change. That was the first time we were on the same page." Bald was quiet for a few seconds and then said, "I still have that shotgun as a reminder."

We sat in silence for a while. I acted like the car was filled with enough noises and activities to forget where I was or what I was supposed do. Bald moved as little as possible. He looked as if he was reflecting on his story. I didn't want to ask follow-up questions, nor did he go on with more. He'd made his point clear to me, and there wasn't time to point out any problems I suspected.

A shadow passed the car, making Bald's head do a quick look in the rearview mirror. He opened the door and quickly got out when I looked into the mirror. Before I could say anything, Ramone was in the passenger seat again. He sat in the seat, unmoving, while Bald took his place directly behind me once more. His white shirt had turned into a Jackson Pollock with blood splattered across from the poor soul he just visited. His face and breathing hadn't changed since he was in the car last. A few seconds went by before Ramone reached into his pocket and pulled out the car keys. When he handed them to me, I noticed the blood on his hand and the keys.

"Get us out of here," Ramone said.

The drive home was just as silent as it was to the apartment building. Most of the drive had me looking at my right hand where some of the keys' smeared blood on it. I kept glancing over just enough before Ramone could tell me to stop and pay attention.

When I got back to my place, Ramone told me to get out and leave the car running. As I got out, Bald jumped into the driver's side. Neither one of them said anything as I stood in the street, watching them burn rubber and leave a trail of smoke.

The first thing I did in my apartment was wash the blood off my hand. Yes, taking pictures with a cell phone to capture this would've been the best option, but I could picture Johns, red faced, telling me how he wasn't going to be tricked as he slapped the handcuffs on me. Also, I didn't have a camera lying around. I scrubbed and scrubbed until I saw skin peeling off. My hand looked like a giant strawberry when I was done.

Afterwards, I spun the dial on the rotary. I was wide awake and didn't want any more surprises for the night without telling someone what happened. I needed the moment while everything was still fresh in my head. The ringing coming from the other end of the line didn't make my head any better. Finally, it stopped and I heard Catherine's tired voice. Before she could say anything, I told her it was me and quickly went into everything that had happened. I could hear her fumbling around, but that didn't stop me from blurting out all the words I needed. She was quiet most of the time, getting in quick questions when she had the chance. I told her I would be in touch with her soon and to back off from doing anything.

After the call with her, once again, I spun the dial for David. This time my plan was to give him only a summary of what had happened, but made sure he was ready for the next step. He didn't sound tired when he picked up, and his voice sounded more like a worried parent.

I said, "Get the camera ready."

15

I took off work the next day, using the morning to help Thelma fix the leaky faucet. Henderson wasn't thrilled with me taking the time off, but I told him I would replace the fluorescent lights in the bathrooms. He felt a little better, and then told me to have a nice day. I had plenty of time before I had to meet the guys for the scheduled taping, and I didn't want to forget my duties around the house. The leaky faucet wasn't a hassle to fix, but I still took my time.

Thelma sat at the kitchen table, eating a bowl of yogurt because it was the easiest thing for her to eat. She's quiet as a mouse when she knows I'm working on any repairs to the house. The only sound I heard was the spoon scraping the ceramic bowl she used to eat her breakfast. She didn't want to feel useless, so I told her before I began to open the drawers underneath the sink and then she hung out in case I needed anything.

Being on my back under the kitchen sink was oddly comforting. This type of easy work gave me time to assess everything in my life that had happened and where things were going. I could interpret last night as killing two birds with one stone: getting done what needed to be done, while also trying to make me understand who's in charge. Maybe they figured I would give up easily by now and tell them I wanted no more of these assignments. What they didn't understand was my commitment to the end—whatever that might be.

I pulled myself from underneath, telling Thelma I was done. She smiled and breathed a sigh of relief.

"Oh, good," she said, wiping her mouth with a paper napkin. "That leak was bothering me the past couple days. Thank you, Truman."

"These are old pipes, but they still have some life in them."

She shuffled to her purse and pulled out a five-dollar bill. "How about you pick me up a bottle of merlot and get yourself something."

I smiled. "Your money is no good to me—I'd be robbing you. I've been meaning to get myself a bottle of bourbon." I checked the clock hanging above the stove. "They should be open by the time I get there. I'll pick you up some merlot."

Once more, she insisted I take the Lincoln bill, but I held up my hands like I was being robbed.

When I got into my car, I did a quick look around to see if anyone had been looking at me longer than they should. I didn't see anything odd at first until I turned my head to the right and focused. A silver Porsche sat about fifty yards down the street. The tinted windows made it difficult to see who was behind the wheel. There was no way I could chase after that machine with my Honda, so I turned on the engine and pretended everything was fine.

On the way to the liquor store, I occasionally looked into the rearview and side-view mirrors for the Porsche. The first half of the trip I didn't notice anything. At an intersection with no sight of the vehicle, I started to go when a pickup truck cut me off, making me slam on my brakes. Just as I gave the roughneck the finger, I saw in the rearview mirror the Porsche, backing up quickly onto the street it was just on. I knew then I wasn't paranoid.

I decided to stick with the plan and go to the liquor store because the place was in a shopping center with plenty of people around. As I pulled into the parking lot, I decided to get a space as close to the store as possible. If I needed to make a sudden getaway, then it wouldn't be a hike to get to my car. I parked next to a sky blue minivan, giving myself a minute to sit in the car and wait for my stalker. After a minute of waiting, and not wanting to look like a stalker myself, I got out.

I had been to that particular liquor and wine store a number of times, so searching for the merlot and bourbon was easy. I wanted to act like I was perusing all the aisles to see if the mystery guest was going to show. The thirty-something Hispanic man behind the counter acted like he regretted his job, so he wasn't paying me any attention. I walked up and down the aisles, pretending to debate what to get, but at the same time, keeping my focus on the front entrance. Except for the door, the front of the store was covered with windows. This gave me enough to see the world moving outside.

Five minutes passed without anything happening. I had already picked up both items I came for. The clerk behind the counter hadn't once looked up at me. The only other person I saw since entering the store five minutes ago was an elderly woman who, surprisingly, looked older than Thelma. If she was a spy for Victoria, then she deserved an award.

I started for the clerk with my two bottles when Vince strolled through the door. The car and man hit me like a train. Only someone with a large bank account would be stupid enough to flash what they had on a stakeout. He already had his sights on me when he stepped through. He had determination in his eyes as he casually made his way to me. He wore everything you shouldn't when following someone: a wool coat, a dark blue polo shirt, dark slacks,

107

and aviators from an unoriginal cop show. I stood there, gripping each bottle.

"Why were you following me?" I asked.

He didn't seem phased. "You are something else. I thought you were serious about finding my sister's killer. You had that beautiful speech prepared for me and I bought into it."

"What are you talking about?"

"I saw you with Ramone and one of his guys last night."

I blinked my eyes in annoyance. "That's not what you think. After talking with you, I searched for Ramone. It took some time, but after I found him I was able to meet up with the boss, Victoria. Have you met her before?"

He shook his head.

"It's a phony name, but she's serious." I eased my hands a little from each bottleneck. "I told her she has someone working for her who murdered Danielle, but she didn't believe it. So I made a deal with her."

Vince squinted. "A deal?"

"I would work a few jobs for her in exchange for information about Danielle and how that connects to her death."

He laughed. "How dumb do you take me for?"

Sweat built up under my collar. Occasionally I would look to see if the clerk bothered to watch us talk since our voices started to get louder. He didn't. No one else, thankfully, had entered the store at that time. Vince wasn't giving me the opportunity to open his mind and show that we were on the same side. I could only go a little bit further with him before giving up and walking out.

I said, "You're not thinking clearly. Why would I talk to you if I had any involvement in Danielle's death? Maybe you only buy drugs from Ramone, but you don't see the danger Ramone and his thugs bring." I adjusted both bottles in my hands. "If you have anything you found, tell me now. I would rather you give me the golden clue now."

He took a few steps back. "I actually thought her murder was somehow related to a dispute with a student. Now I see the people I thought were on my side are actually against me. Did all of you murder her because of the fifteen grand I owe? Well, I got your message, and now you can go back and tell them I'll be waiting for them."

After giving the last statement, Vince bolted out of the store. Now I had to put him on the list of things I should be worried about. There was nothing I could say that he would want to hear— or believe. His warpath was built on misunderstandings and false allegations. There had to be some way to neutralize him without turning violent. The problem was he didn't see it that way. His anger was my anger, but I wanted to know everything before exacting justice.

The clerk had finally given me his attention as I approached the counter. I could only hope he hadn't heard too much of that conversation, and I wasn't going to ask what he overheard. His brown eyes had a neutral look to them as he rang up both bottles. His facial expression showed he didn't care. He fumbled a little putting both bottles in a brown paper bag. When he handed me my change and receipt, he tried his best to give me a smile. I smiled back and went on my way.

Outside, the sun was doing a good job of warming things up. I stood on the sidewalk, looking to see if the Porsche was still in the area. My guess was Vince parked it at the farthest end of the lot because he knew I would spot him through the windows if he got too close. Even with him fumbling on everything else, he did have some sense. This explains why none of us spotted him last night.

I had to get to Goliath's place soon because David told me

last night, in our quick conversation, that he would be busy, but to go to Goliath's and he would help me out. I hadn't talked to Goliath that morning, but David said he would catch him up with everything and that I would be expected. Adding Vince to the mix would be newsworthy for Goliath to hear. As I took a step off the sidewalk, a recognizable, annoying voice shouted from my right.

"So glad I was able to run into you."

Detective Johns wobbled down the sidewalk towards me. He wasn't wearing his normal wrinkled tied or stained white-collar shirt. Instead, he wore a flannel shirt and jeans. It was either his day off or he was ready to do undercover work in an Indiana factory. He hurried his pace when he saw me starting for my car.

"Now you wait there a minute," he said, catching his breath. "I need to talk to you."

"I'm not in the mood today."

He poked my shoulder. "Well, I'm in the mood, and you're going to listen to me, son."

I didn't move. My only choice was to stand like a statue until he got his big-boy threats out of the way. I could already see the sweat building up on him and it wasn't that hot out.

"Already wasting your day away?" he asked as he looked into the paper bag I carried.

"Just picking up some items for my landlady. Is that a crime now?"

He shook his head. "It's not, but we're making great progress on the Hutchins' killing. I can't go into specifics right now, but all I can say is you better not flee town or I'm personally coming after you. No place on God's earth can you hide from me."

I gave a small snort.

"You may have my partner and everyone else fooled, but I know you had your hand in her death."

"Or maybe you did?" I blurted.

"What was that?"

"Nothing. Am I under arrest, or did you seriously think harassing me would do anything?"

Johns started to talk again, but I walked away from more verbal threats. He had started to get under my skin, and my filter wasn't on. Johns was waiting for me to reply, to let something slip. I wouldn't give him the satisfaction. Even with him shouting after me, I didn't glance back over my shoulder. The circles I was going with Johns were only giving me headaches.

On the way to Goliath's, I was trying to make sense about Vince and Johns. It was clear Vince was following, but seeing Johns like that out of the blue made me think he was doing the same. Each had their suspicions with me and wanted to make sure I was on a short leash. Vince wanted to get right to the point, while Johns wanted to put enough pressure on me to slip. Thinking about both of their intentions gave me a headache.

Goliath's place was similar to mine. He also lived in the basement, but his landlords were his parents. The neighborhood was your typical American Dream-style setup: two-story house, white picket fence, and grass that wasn't allowed to be higher than a few inches. It wasn't difficult to find, but I didn't feel comfortable having so many prying eyes from nosy neighbors as I exited my car. An unfamiliar face can be worse than Freddy Krueger.

Goliath saw me get out of my car and walk up to his place. He was in the back corner, waving me to go around the house and follow him. David already told me Goliath's parents wouldn't be home.

The layout to a college man still living with his parents was mostly how I pictured it. He had heavy-metal posters on the walls— some I know, most I've never heard of. There was a bathroom to the left when you walked in, and the kitchen across from there. There were plenty of crumbs lying on the counters for a family of mice to have a feast, and dishes stacked higher than the Eiffel Tower. The room down the hall with a door open looked like his room. Next to the kitchen were more computers and gizmos than NASA could concoct. I thought how high the electric bill must be to power the station.

This was where Goliath led me. There were four computer monitors sitting on a desk, and in front of them were two black leather chairs. When we sat down, I could see on Goliath's face how he didn't have people around his place often. He was fidgety, looking for the right questions to ask when you have a guest.

"Can I get you something to drink?" he asked.

"No, I'm fine right now." I looked around at his digital kingdom. "How can you afford all this stuff?"

He looked around like he was impressed, too. "I'm not going to lie; my parents helped me out some. I've also had part-time jobs and people giving me good discounts." He rolled his chair over to a desk with a number of gadgets and wires laying on top. "David told me you had an eventful night."

"One way of putting it. There are plenty of details I need to get recorded that would fill a memory card."

Goliath half-listened as he shifted through everything on the desk. He would whisper loud enough for me to hear but not enough for him to care. Each drawer he opened up and knocked around, cursing as he moved to the next one. It wasn't until the bottom drawer that he gave a sigh of relief. He pulled out a video recorder. It was slightly older than what David had, but he didn't care as long as it got the job done.

"Is that one of David's recorders?" I asked.

He rolled back to me. "No, but this one works the same. What he and I can do later is splice the videos together to make one file instead of jumping back and forth."

Goliath fidgeted with the device, trying to make sure everything was set with no interruptions. I wasn't wearing my neutral face because his eyes were showing sorrow.

"Can you still keep going with everything?" he asked.

"I can, but the weight is getting to me."

"What happened last night?"

"I'll wait for the camera. I'm not exactly in the mood to say it more than once."

Goliath indicated the camera was ready. He told me to wait another minute as he set up a tripod on the desk so it wouldn't appear shaky. We weren't making a big-budget motion picture, but I just sat there while he developed his peace of mind. When he finally got things set up, I leaned forward, running through everything I wanted to get down. He stopped himself from hitting the record button.

He said, "I want to come along with you the next time you go out."

I quickly shook my head. "These are not field trips I'm doing. I stepped into something I can't clean off my shoe. They're not going to slow down if they know how many people are with me."

"But you look like you need the backup."

"And that's what I'm doing with the help you and David are already giving me."

"I could—"

"What? You could do what? Trying to trick this group wouldn't go smoothly. I don't even know everyone who is working for Victoria. What I do know is that we're walking through a minefield at night with a glow stick." I rested my face and calmed down a little. "Maybe when David can get his miniature spy device working I'll consider adjusting the plan, but until then I'm going with what I said."

Goliath added nothing as he turned on the camera. He told me I could begin.

I must've talked around thirty minutes. I kept pushing myself to make sure everything I had to say was out there. When I got to the part about Victoria's deep pockets, I glanced over at Goliath. Maybe it was the unknown lackeys who worked for her, or maybe I didn't have any evidence to back up her claim, or maybe I just didn't feel like saying it in the moment, but I left out that part of my story. Up until then I was talking like a teenage girl after her first date. I censored myself, knowing full well it was only hurting me. When Goliath went to open his mouth, I continued the rest of the story. After a few more minutes, I signaled I was done by exhaling.

Goliath's hand hovered over the camera. "Is that all?"

I nodded.

He pressed a button on top of the camera and the red light went out. Slowly, he took the camera off the tripod and set the machine next to a silver laptop on the desk. He opened a different drawer and put the tripod away. Without saying a word, he took the recorder and sat in his chair facing away from me. I rolled my chair closer as he turned on one of the computer screens. He took one of the wires coming from the desktop and connected it to the recorder's port. His eyes moved rapidly as he clicked on a bunch of screens and then rushed to upload my testimony.

"Are you making a copy on your desktop?" I asked.

"Making a copy on the desktop, but also putting a copy in the Cloud. David did the same with your first video. We want to make sure that if anything happens to us they won't be able to erase every copy they get their hands on."

I sat back against the chair with ease. "Not a bad idea."

"I have it set so that if anything happens to me, it gets sent to every corner of the internet."

I studied the computer screen. "Have you been able to find anything about Victoria or Danielle's death?"

He turned to me, shaking his head. "An operation of this size in our small town should have been all over the police reports and the internet, but it's been minimal. Sure, the few arrests from Ramone showed up, but besides that, it hasn't been much. What I'm afraid of is that there might be a few corrupt cops brushing this under the rug and letting Victoria get away."

I let what was supposed to be unproven scare tactics hit me in the face. Victoria might've gotten into my head with her statement, but the evidence was now before me. Victoria wouldn't easily give up her contacts in the police department. It was difficult to trust cops like Eagle Scout Longhorn. Still, I thought putting Goliath in the know at this point would help me more.

I said, "There's something I need to tell you."

He turned, studying my face.

I went over everything Victoria had told me about owning a significant amount of the police force. I told him I thought it was a way for her to put fear in me, but that it was becoming more evident. I explained that she wouldn't give me a number of how many cops were on her payroll, but that it was enough for her to get away all of this time. Goliath didn't say one word as I talked. It was more of a summary of what I knew, but his face told me how stupefied he was. After I was done, we sat there for another minute, letting the gravity wrap around our minds.

"Why didn't you say anything before?" he asked.

"I don't have a simple answer. I started this because of Danielle's death, but now I'm dealing with corrupt cops and drug dealers.

The more I know, the bigger the target on my back becomes." I looked him right in the eyes. "And now you know, making you a target."

"And that is why you need to put that on camera. Everything we do should be made clear to the world just in case something happens." He tapped the armrest of his seat with his index finger. "As for me, I understand the full risk of what you're telling me."

Without having to tell him, Goliath reached for his recorder, and then went through the drawer for the tripod. This time he was quicker in setting up the camera. I didn't move, sitting in the chair perfectly calm.

When he pressed the red button again, I wasted no time in adding to my testimony. Instead of giving the same summary I told Goliath, I went into detail with everything from the moment Victoria told me her power structure within the police department to the new evidence we discovered. To Goliath's shock, I mentioned his name and said how we were going to link this video with the police reports for the past year that looked like law enforcement redacted certain information or didn't file anything. Goliath turned off the camera.

"That information I showed you was from me hacking into the department's system," he said. His hands were folded as if he were ready to pray. "That will backfire and it won't be used as evidence."

"True, but we can put this out there for everyone to see. That could be the start for a number of people to find the whole truth." I kept going when Goliath still didn't look convinced. "Ok, you said this information would only be used if something happens to us. You can edit out the last part and withhold what you found in the department's system if everything turns out fine."

Goliath was still hesitant, but he nodded his approval.

He turned the camera back on, giving me another minute to

wrap up what I had to say with a nice bow.

When everything was officially done with the recording, Goliath uploaded the new part into the desktop. His typing and computer skills were faster this time, like the cops were about to burst through the door if he didn't get it uploaded fast enough. He was about halfway done when I picked myself up off the chair and started for the door.

I said, "All right, I'll be in touch soon."

"You aren't going to wait for David? He should be here shortly."

"Nah, I'll see him soon. I think I gave enough talk for now. Show him everything I recorded today and everything you found to catch him up. I want both you guys to be on board with everything."

He said, "I will."

16

For the rest of the evening, I let quietness and loneliness be my friends. I had checked on Thelma after getting home with the merlot. She was grateful for all of the liquid cheer she could still experience at her age. I asked if there were any problems with the kitchen sink, but she shook her head and thanked me again for repairing the pipe. I let her know that if she needed anything, I would be around for the night.

As the dying light of the day shone its orange rays through the small windows of my apartment, I played the Duke, Miles, Louis, and every record I owned to bring some life in for a change. Lying down, I would tap my fingers against my chest to keep the rhythm going. I let the melodies help me focus on the areas I could use as an advantage against Victoria and her crime wave. Instead of letting her put the fear of God in me, I could use the little time she let me have to throw everything back at her.

Instead of eating fruit out of a can for dinner, I whipped up some enchiladas with a side of meatballs. These weren't items you would find together as an entrée on a restaurant menu, but a single man can get creative when his stomach is roaring. The prepping and cooking distracted me from thinking about everything—a rarity I enjoyed. The dinner came out perfect to me. After a full stomach, I still had plenty of leftovers for the next few days.

I spent the last few moments of the waking night sitting on the couch. Another record played while I put my list together of cops I knew who could be looking to silence me. Sure, Johns was the easiest suspect for anyone to put high on the list, but I was worried about cops with a nice smile and itchy trigger fingers. Longhorn might seem like that type, but he had been smart enough to back off when things started to heat up.

I didn't know what time I fell asleep, but it was a little after midnight when the footsteps outside startled me awake. I froze for a few seconds, making sure what I was hearing wasn't coming from an animal or the house playing games with me. The footsteps were soft, nothing like I had heard before when Ramone or Bald showed up. I followed the sound that moved against the wall outside. The darkness hid the mystery guest well, even when they were close to the house. Carefully, I kept low so the stranger didn't know my whereabouts.

I moved gradually towards the door. The switch to the light outside hadn't been working for months, and it wasn't exactly high on my list of things to repair. I had to get the jump on them before they could get it on me. I stood off to the side of the door, hand on the doorknob. I realized I should've gotten anything as a weapon, but I couldn't risk making any more noise. I listened as the sound grew louder and louder. When I heard the person only inches from my door, I swung it open.

Catherine filled the doorway, face covered in blood. Both of her hands were on opposite sides of the doorframe, holding herself up. She looked at me with tired eyes glazed with blood. She opened her mouth to speak, but all that came out were red bubbles. I caught her before she could collapse to the ground.

Lifting her up, I carried her over to my couch and then gently laid her down. A roll of paper towels were the closest thing I could reach to start wiping the blood away from her face. Her eyes were shut, going in and out of consciousness. When I thought she had passed out for good, I went straight to the rotary. Just as I picked up the receiver, I heard a sound just loud enough for me to hear.

"No hospital," said Catherine.

Reluctantly, I put the phone back on the cradle. I went into the bathroom to pick out gauze and every bandage I could find. I even grabbed every clean towel to help with the bleeding. I carried everything out to her like I couldn't make a second trip.

For twenty minutes, I did my best to dress the wounds and to clean up the blood. There were several cuts and bruises across her face and head. There was a cut coming from her forehead that was responsible for the blood in her eyes. I couldn't tell whether the cuts were deep enough for stitches. I covered them up with bandages. If any of her wounds became infected, she wouldn't have a choice. Later, when she was conscious again and able to see a doctor about the injuries, I would explain to her about the bandages.

I sat with her for an hour, making sure there weren't any changes to her condition. I checked every few minutes to monitor her breathing and to feel for a pulse. I planned to stay like this all night. The image of her, half dead, on my couch was exactly what I feared. People like me ran into the bear's den, thinking the situation was under control, but in reality, there was honey covered all over it. Just as I was starting to get tired again, Catherine started waking up.

"Where am I?" she asked. It was hard to understand what she was saying, but it was audible enough.

I moved myself so she could see me. "It's Truman. You're at my place."

She tried sitting up, but that only made her moan. Her shoulders on the armrest was as far as she could go. She gently moved her legs as I took my place on the other end. Her left eye was closed, leaving her right eye to look at me. I let her take in her reality for a moment before continuing.

"What happened?" I asked.

"Could I get a glass of water?"

In one of the cabinets above the kitchen sink, I picked out the last clean glass and filled it with tap water. When I handed the cup over to her I made sure she had the strength to hold the cup by herself. She sipped the water, giving a relaxed exhale as she held the cup with both hands. Her eyes moved around the room for a minute, looking as if she was still piecing together the puzzle in her head. She finally met my eyes.

She said, "I took things into my own hands and decided I could help with Danielle's death. I couldn't just sit by and let you run around like a cowboy."

She coughed and a little blood landed on her hand. Her head shook when I started to ask if she wanted me to get her anything.

"Brewer's," she continued, "from what you told me, sounded like the best place to begin my search. I had gone there closer to closing time because I felt the place would be dying down and maybe I would get lucky with finding Victoria—or someone close. I sat in my car outside the bar for a long time. I didn't have much of a plan, nor anything if things turned bad. I got out and started towards the bar, figuring it would just come to me."

"So, I took a seat at the bar. I didn't recognize anyone and ultimately started a conversation with the bartender. He didn't seem to mind with the first couple of questions I had 'cause he probably thought he had a shot with me. It wasn't until I asked for Victoria that his face changed. His smile couldn't mask what his eyes were telling me. He told me she was actually in, and he pointed to the back where she was supposedly having a conversation."

"And you didn't think to get out at that moment?" I asked.

"No. I figured the damage was already done when I asked about Victoria. It was a risk to just sit there, and my legs were too wobbly to outrun anyone."

She had a point there. Someone running in a situation like that only means they're up to something. I thought about my first time going to Brewer's the night Danielle died, trying to imitate Clint Eastwood. Not exactly the most subtle way to gain information, and I saw the results right away.

I said, "What happened next?"

"The bartender told me to hang on for a minute as he wanted to see if Victoria was busy. The place, at this point, didn't have anyone in there, so I could see if anyone tried to sneak up on me." She laughed a little. "The loneliness in the moment scared me more. The bartender came back from the hallway, still holding onto the same smile. He told me she was off the phone and could speak to me for a minute. He pointed back down the hall and instructed me to go all the way to the end.

"I knocked on the door, and instead of hearing a woman's voice, I heard a man's voice saying to come in. When I entered, the only person in the room was a man with blond hair."

It was going to be difficult not to rip out Blond's throat the next time I saw him.

"He sat at a poker table by himself. I asked him where Victoria was because I was told she would be here. He told me she hadn't been here and wouldn't be coming. That was when I slowly backed up towards the door, trying to escape. I don't know how I didn't hear it click, but the door was locked. I panicked and faced the handle, trying my best to move it. When I turned again, he was only a few inches away from me. Before I could scream, he had his arms around me and threw me into the poker table. I tried kicking and punching him, but nothing was working. He slugged me a number of times."

It was then she lifted her bloody shirt some to reveal the bruises on her stomach. I looked at the black and blue, wondering how she was even alive.

"I don't know how long it went on for, but it felt like an eternity." Her voice started to crack, making her stop. She lowered her head. A few moments passed before she had the strength for her eyes to meet mine. "During the beating, I couldn't take it anymore and blurted out your name. He thought there was more I knew, so he kept hitting me. When he tired himself out, he got right into my face and told me to give you a message." She waited for a few seconds for me to react, but I let my stone-cold face tell her to continue. "He said for you not to play anymore tricks nor send your assistant. He wants you to do as you're told. Anything more like this and more people will get hurt—the kind you don't get up from again."

I nodded. "And what happened next?"

"He picked me up and threw me into the alley. It took me several minutes to get to my feet. I thought the thug would be back either to check on me or to beat me up some more, so I limped out of the alley as quickly as possible. There wasn't anyone out at the time, so I didn't have to answer questions I might regret. My only luck was that the car wasn't parked far. When I made it, I drove here."

She sniffled a little, but she refused when I offered her a tissue. By the time she was finished, she looked more exhausted. Having to recount a story like that took an emotional toll. Her one good eye forced itself to stay open like she had more to tell me. Her whole body slid back down into the couch.

"Would you like to sleep on my bed and I'll take the couch?"

I asked.

Both eyes were closed while her mouth moved. "No, this couch is quite comfortable."

I went into the closet for a blanket and a pillow so she didn't have to use the wooden armrest. When I returned, she was passed out again. Gently, I put the pillow under her head. I didn't think an earthquake could wake her up. After I put the blanket on her, I checked to see if there was any more bleeding coming from her head. Satisfied, I retired to my bedroom.

I woke up multiple times during the night. Sleep was already nonexistent to me the past few days, but I had the sense someone would try to break in and take out Catherine. All the locks were on and the windows were tightly shut, but that still didn't give me the satisfaction that everything would be ok. Having them know about Catherine further unsettled my mind.

The next morning I woke up just as the sun started to show itself through the windows. Another night of sleeplessness, but I didn't want to sit in the living room and scare Catherine when she got up.

It seemed I overthought the whole thing, because I found Catherine sitting up on the couch. She already had the blanket folded and the pillow on top. She turned to me when my footsteps were loud enough. The swelling on her face had ballooned in certain spots. I could only imagine how many of those would turn into scars. She already had an answer for me when she turned my way.

"It looks worse than it feels," she said. "I took a look at myself a little while ago and was just as surprised as you."

"Did you take any of the Advil in the medicine cabinet?"

She nodded. "Yeah, I didn't want to wake you, and I know my way around a place once I'm settled."

I opened the refrigerator and pretended it was fully stock. "Do you want anything to eat or drink?"

"No, I'm not hungry or thirsty right now."

I sat next to her on the couch, studying her face. Maybe it didn't hurt her, but those injuries weren't going away anytime soon. If she didn't think she needed to go to the doctor's, then I wasn't going to push. Instead, I went over the game plan for the day.

"I'm going into work today," I told her.

She gave me a puzzled look but didn't say anything.

I continued, "I haven't been in for a while and thought today would be a good time to make an appearance while you rested. No one will be around here to bother you."

"I agree. I was going to ask you about staying here for the day while I thought about what to do next."

I smiled. "Good. I had a whole speech planned about why you shouldn't be wandering all over town right now."

"Can you do me a favor?"

"Sure."

"Grab some food on your way back later."

17

Work had gone faster than I thought it would. When I walked in, Henderson couldn't remember if he saw me yesterday or last month. He had no problem remembering the long list of work that I had to get done, though. None of that bothered me, because it would keep my mind on something other than Death knocking on my door. I did the normal routine of scrubbing toilets, mopping floors, and emptying out the waste bins.

During the day, I didn't see the usual suspects. David and Goliath didn't make an appearance, and I didn't think Catherine would be around for a long time—or ever. Even dimwit Kevin hadn't shown his face for a while. There was a calming relaxation all day while I worked that I hadn't felt for some time. I kept to myself for the work shift, and I didn't think I would miss anything of importance. I ate my lunch while Henderson tried to solve a word puzzle. He probably forgot I was sitting in the same room with the amount of cursing he was doing. That afternoon was pretty much the same as the morning.

The atmosphere surrounding Danielle's death had started to subside. Sure, there were some students and faculty still reeling from her death, but everyone seemed to be moving on. One of the secretaries told me her classroom was already being used and that they were about to begin the process of finding a replacement for her. I didn't know how to feel about it. There wasn't much sting to it, nor did it make me happy that they were moving on from her. My only option was to take a neutral stance.

After clocking out for the day, I was walking to my car in the mostly empty parking lot when the silver Porsche was back. This time Vince didn't try to hide his presence. The sun was in the middle of setting, but Vince still let the high beams of the vehicle point in my direction. The engine started to roar when Vince caught sight of me.

I took a dozen steps towards his car, not letting the sly sleuth think he had any power over me. I stopped about a hundred feet away from the car, not even opening my mouth to challenge him. He wanted to try a scare tactic, and I was more than willing to call his bluff. I kept my stance in the middle of asphalt island, waiting for him to make the next move.

Just when I thought he was going to back up, he put the car in drive and sped towards me. I stood my ground as he moved with incredible haste. Just as he was about to hit me, he turned the car just enough that he missed me by inches. He started doing doughnuts, circling me like a hawk would with its prey. The smoke he produced flowed all around me. The first time he circled me, we looked directly at each other. In those few seconds, our eyes pierced through each other, determined to show the other person why they were wrong. After the fourth circle around me, he sped off to the main road.

As a way to give him a message, I picked up a rock the size of a golf ball and chucked it at the car. It hit the trunk, causing the machine to brake. I kept my face on the Porsche, unmoving while the beast roared. If he was going to hit me, then I wanted it to be over with quickly. We had a staring contest that lasted a few seconds. The brake lights disappeared and the machine was gone before the smoke cleared.

On the way home I decided to stop at a fast food place instead of a market. I knew Catherine wanted a home-cooked meal, but my stomach and mind weren't in that area. I stopped at a place called Harry's to order some burgers and fries. Waiting in the drive-thru also gave me the time to make sure Vince didn't want to keep the games going in a different parking lot. I didn't see him, but I knew he wouldn't be gone for long.

When I got back to my place, there was a feeling Catherine would be long gone when I opened the door. But when I stepped through, she was sitting on the couch with her feet up. There was joy in her face when she saw me.

"I haven't had Harry's in a long time," she said, looking at the bag in my hand.

I put the bag on the kitchen table. "Neither have I. Thought it would be perfect for tonight."

Catherine didn't say anything more as she sat at the kitchen table with me, going through the fries and opening the burger wrapper. I quickly cleaned two glass cups and filled them with some tap, handing one off to her.

"Did you have any problems hiding out here today?" I asked.

"No. There weren't any visitors. I thought your landlady might stop by, but she didn't." She smirked. "You live a lonely life."

"Well, it hasn't been lonely for a while now. All this excitement can last me a lifetime."

She bit into her cheeseburger. "Did anything happen today?"

I shook my head. "No, pretty calm."

I didn't want to tell her about Vince yet because I wasn't sure where things were going with him. He wanted to play cowboy, but that's all the commotion he was causing so far. We already had enough to worry about with Victoria and her gang, so telling

Catherine that a man was making a bunch of noise didn't make sense.

Catherine and I had both just finished eating when I started to clear the table. I threw away the wrappers and the bag into the trash bin under the kitchen sink. I started to reach for the glasses when we heard footsteps coming from outside. Catherine whipped her face towards the door like it had already been kicked in. We sat in silence to see if the footsteps were going away or coming closer. When it was determined they were for us, Catherine whispered she was going to hide in the bathroom. She was already halfway there when I nodded in acceptance.

I opened the door before they could knock. Ramone stood in front once again, but this time Blond, not Bald, was the extra leash to be dragged along. I tried to step out with them, but they pushed past me and entered my place. It didn't seem like they were in a hurry this time.

"I guess you already know why we're here," said Ramone.

I gave a disappointed look. "I do."

"There's something we need to talk about."

Ramone might've been the one talking, but it was Blond I focused on. Every time I looked at him, he had a shit-eating grin on that I wanted to wipe off. It was clear he was brought to test my patience. Under the left side of his leather jacket was a gun—not sure what type—ready to fire the bullet that would end me. They knew they wanted a reason to make sure I didn't come back home tonight. All I was to them was a fly in the ointment, and they were looking to squash the bug for good. This still didn't distract me for imagining all the different ways I was going to teach Blond what it felt like when someone stronger knocks you around.

Ramone motioned to Blond. "I was told that one of your associates foolishly thought it was a good idea to stop by Brewer's last night." He waited for me to say something, but I stood my ground. "There is nothing you can do to change what is going to happen. Sending someone on a meaningless errand like that will only get more people hurt. We know you are trying any trick you can do, but it's futile. The next time you send someone, we will lay the corpse at your doorstep."

If he was expecting a response from me, he wasn't going to get one. I made myself pretend to think about everything he said, but I didn't care. What he didn't understand was there were other people just as determined as me to find the truth. I wasn't going out and recruiting anyone, nor did I have to convince anyone to help me. Ramone looked at me with anger, but Blond threw his eyes to the kitchen table.

"Were you really thirsty or something?" asked Blond.

I didn't know what he was talking about until he pointed to the table. I had cleared everything except for the two glasses—each half full.

I said, "My landlady was just down here and I was cleaning up." I had to say something before either of them asked more questions.

"How romantic," said Blond.

I ignored that. "Can we get going now?"

"Before we go," said Blond, making his way to the bathroom, "I've got to drain the lizard."

Jumping up and saying "no" in the moment would only draw skepticism. The only thing I could do was prepare myself for a fight. I figured the second he opened the door and spotted Catherine, I would have to make a jump for Ramone. My only chance would be Ramone's curiosity lowering his guard long enough for me to attack. I didn't have time to pick up any weapon around me. It would come down to a wrestling match for the concealed gun in his back waistband. Then it would be a matter of getting to Blond before he could do more harm to Catherine.

I slightly turned my feet towards Ramone just as Blond opened the door and walked into the bathroom. For the first few seconds I leaned towards Ramone, waiting for the cue to make my move. But as the time went on and I could hear Blond pissing into the toilet without saying a word, I let myself cool down. Catherine was either hiding well in the bathroom or she'd made it out somehow. It had to be the latter, which made me coolly look around the apartment for her. I couldn't let Ramone know what I was doing, so I would pretend to check the time or do something that made him think I was putting my senses on objects that didn't concern him.

Blond walked out of the bathroom without washing his hands. "Now I'm ready."

I didn't want them in my place anymore, so I walked out without grabbing anything. Even with the chill in the air, I didn't feel like I needed a jacket.

I held my hand out to Ramone for the car keys. For the first time, I saw Ramone give me a half-smile as he took the keys out of his pocket. I would make sure to get them as far—and as fast— away from my place as I could.

18

We did the whole *Driving Miss Daisy* routine again, but this time with Ramone sitting in the back and Blond in the passenger seat. The leather seat felt cooler than the last time. My hands had a tighter grip around the steering wheel. I kept putting more pressure on the gas than I should, which led to Blond repeatedly reminding me to slow down before the cops got us before we got the job done.

From time to time I kept checking the rearview mirrors for any sign of Vince. I had the sense he had been following even before we got in the car. An opportunity like this would be perfect for him to throw the monkey wrench into the motor. Headlights popped up now and again, but those belonged to anything but a Porsche. I didn't realize I was constantly looking until Ramone spoke up.

"Do you see something?" he asked.

I kept my focus forward. "No. I thought I saw a cop, but it was nobody."

Maybe it was the satisfaction of getting the goons away from Catherine, but the drive didn't feel like it took long to get to our destination. There weren't any backroads this time, nor anything that would make us look conspicuous to ordinary people. It took less than twenty minutes in total for Ramone to point out where we needed to go. He did his usual, telling me when to turn and how far to go.

The destination turned out to be a residential neighborhood one doesn't venture into at night. Bountiful Springs, or as people called it "Blood Springs," was the epicenter for drugs and weapons entering the area. I wasn't fully shocked when Ramone made me turn into the cesspool. Even though this neighborhood wasn't far from where I lived, I had never stepped foot in this place before.

Driving through I could see the eyes of the curious people, looking at who would be dumb enough to ride through. When I was going down the main drag, there were a number of kids playing basketball in the middle of the street. They all started to walk towards the headlights like they were going to buy the car from us for free. When most of them saw who the car belonged to, they parted like the Red Sea. An obese kid with curly brown hair was about to throw the basketball at the car until a lanky kid with dreads dragged him out of the way.

Our final destination was a one-story, light blue siding house towards the end of the road. By the time I parked across the street and cut the engine, there was no one in sight, except for the curious eyes hiding behind the windows and fences. When the car was off, all I could hear was the wind pass by.

Ramone got out, holding out his hand to me for the keys. I obliged.

The owner of the house must've thought Ramone was going to show up later because I saw a number of lights turning on, shadows running across the windows. Just as Ramone reached the door, it swung open in a cartoony way. It was difficult to see the face, but the outline was an obese man. He tripped over himself as he moved out of the way for Ramone to walk in, and then closed the door.

Awkward silences are normally interrupted by someone who can't stand the uncomfortableness. I am usually that person when I'm at a social gathering. I didn't want the silence broken between me and the abusive asshole to my right. At first, Blond would cough or scratch his face to remind me he was still in the car. If he wanted me to say something, he was out of luck. I kept my focus on the house. I was hoping Ramone would be out any second, and I didn't want to listen to Blond tell me a story as a way to intimidate me. It didn't last long.

"Do you kn—"

"How long will Ramone be?" I asked.

Blond laughed. "Why? Do you have to meet up with that sneaky bitch?"

I closed my eyes. Didn't matter what angle I tried to play this, Blond was only going to circle back around. "Did he say?"

Blond slowly whistled. "After I beat that dumb bitch and threw her out, my first thought was of your cowardice. Using a woman to sneak your way into cracking us down was low. How much did you pay her?" From the corner of my eyes I could see him smirking. "Or did you pay her in other ways?"

I didn't answer.

"How are you feeling now that your grand scheme blew up in your face?"

I didn't answer.

"Do you know what I'm going to do when you send that tasty bitch again?"

I started to ball my fists.

"I'm going to make sure she won't ever come out with another self-centered idea again. I'm going to throw her face down on the poker table. Then I'm going to rip every piece of clothing off her. If she bleeds, it will only make me harder. And th—"

My elbow connected with his nose, causing his head to snap back against the headrest. I used both of my fists to throw everything I had against his face and chest. Instead of hitting or blocking me, he reached under his jacket for his gun.

"It's about time," he said. Blood poured out of his nose, but he smiled.

I quickly grabbed both of his arms, trying to restrain him as much as possible. My left arm slipped, giving him the two seconds he needed to pull the nine millimeter Glock. I was able to punch him in the face again with my right. When his head hit against the window, I turned both of my hands to his arm holding the weapon.

As I struggled to take the gun away, a faint light appeared behind us. As the seconds passed, the light became stronger. I could see from the corner of my eye it was getting brighter. Neither Blond nor I stopped to check what was happening. We didn't have to deal with this new factor until the car carrying the lights hit the backside of the Charger. Blond and I went forward, me hitting my head against the steering wheel.

"Goddamn it!" said Blond.

I turned my head to see the Porsche backing up but staying on my side of the car. Vince's front left side was messed up, but that didn't slow the machine down at all. It moved like there wasn't a scratch on the car. Between the nighttime and the tinted windows of the Porsche, I couldn't see Vince behind the wheel.

Blond put our fight on pause as he opened his door and jumped out of his seat onto the sidewalk. I didn't want to jump out onto the road so I could be hit by Vince, and I didn't want to remind Blond I was still here. He didn't waste any time lifting his gun and firing it at the Porsche. Vince reversed the car, swerving all over the road in the process.

Blond, screaming, stood in the middle of the road. He unloaded the rest of his magazine at the car. I thought Vince was hit because the car sat in the middle of the street for a few seconds, but it wasn't until Blond reloaded that the engine started to roar, still sitting in place. Blond also stood in the middle of the road like he was the untouchable gunslinger. Even with his arm raised and a new clip in the gun, he wouldn't fire. The two stared at each other for a few seconds, then Vince stepped on the gas. The car moved faster than Blond was prepared for. He started firing the gun when the car was halfway towards him, hitting the windshield and hood. With the car barreling down on him, Blond wouldn't move an inch. He was confident he could hit Vince right through the head like John Wayne. This dream disappeared when Blond hit the windshield, rolled over the car, and smashed onto the ground.

Time was precious, so I quickly got out of the car and went up to Blond's body. Covered in blood, I searched Blond and the surrounding area for his gun. I had my back to Vince's car, keeping an ear on where he was. I was about to give up when I saw the gun sitting in a patch of grass, roughly fifteen feet away from the body. I did a leaping action to get the gun. When my hands touched the gun, I was ready for my defense, but a voice spoke behind me.

"Drop the gun and get up, Truman."

When I did, Vince stood right next to Blond's body. He wasn't far from his car—a quick exit. He smiled as he lifted a .45 automatic at me.

"I knew it," he said.

He started to pull the trigger when a loud cough sounded. We both looked at Blond as the bloody figure tried to crawl away from us. Vince laughed. Lowering the gun from me, he pointed the weapon to Blond and fired. Half of Blond's head exploded, and the other half turned to orange.

Vince quickly turned the gun back on me. Just as he put his finger on the trigger, a small explosion hit him in the shoulder. I looked to see Ramone standing in the front entrance with his smoking Beretta. Vince ran to his car, aimlessly firing in Ramone's direction. All of his shots hit the house or went through the window—none coming close to the intended target. I used this distraction to run back to the Charger. Vince held onto his shoulder as he jumped back into the Porsche, reversing like he was going to drive all the way home that way.

Like we were in sync, I jumped into the passenger seat, and Ramone, keys and gun out, found the driver's side. He made a one-eighty turn, smoke everywhere, and hightailed it down the street. On the way out, a number of people stayed in their homes, the same routine, I imagined, they experienced daily. I imagined it would be some time before the cops showed, but that still wasn't going to stop us from getting the hell out of there.

The way back was completely silent. Unlike the talkative Blond, Ramone didn't say a word, but everything he wanted to express he was doing through body language. His anger was palpable the way he gripped the steering wheel, hands turning red and white as he wouldn't let go. His eyes didn't seem to blink the entire time. Ramone even took the backroads to make sure nothing else happened. He kept the speed limit down to a reasonable speed, but the damaged back of the car spelled suspicion for any curious cop.

Ramone let me out at the end of my street, practically driving off before I was fully out of the car. He didn't say anything about what would happen next as he sped off. The only sound I heard came from the tires screeching.

The quarter-mile or so it took to walk back to my place was filled with enough thoughts to give anyone an aneurysm. I felt numb for everything I saw, but I wanted to think of the next steps before my mind crashed. The thought of Catherine didn't even occur to me until I was halfway back. I forgot she had been there when I left. Nothing like a homicide to make you forget a woman who was beaten to an inch of her life was hiding out at your place.

I searched the entire apartment for Catherine when I got back. After I rushed through the basement door, I first checked the bathroom. I kept yelling her name when she didn't appear like Houdini. I didn't care if I woke up Thelma. Now wasn't the time for Catherine to go into hiding nor to think she could take them on again—if that's where her mind went. I checked under my bed, went through the coat closet, and even checked the refrigerator after getting a beer. My guess was she didn't stay long after we left.

Instead of spinning the numbers on the rotary, I took my usual spot at the kitchen table. I chugged down the whole beer, letting the bottle drop to the floor when I was done. I tried to think about Catherine, Vince, or the guys, but my mind could only picture red. Seeing brains and blood scattered all over the road would be a mental image that stuck with me for a long time. I understood there was a strong chance I wouldn't make it out, but that's what I accepted. I didn't want any more bloodshed, but I was the fly telling the rhino to be better.

I didn't want to think anymore. Back in the bathroom I stepped into the tub, fully clothed, and turned on the shower head. I couldn't even remember what the temperature the water was that sprayed on me. I lay down where the shower head would be directed towards my chest. I tried a breathing technique a masseuse I once dated taught me, but that ended with me screaming. The only time I laughed was when I actually thought for a second I could come up with a plan to outmaneuver everyone and walk away with my life.

Time had eluded me. You could've walked through my apartment and stolen any of the garbage I owned and I wouldn't have budged. Ramone kicking in my door and putting a bullet in my head would be doing me more favors.

Seconds? Minutes? Hours? I wasn't sure as my hands covered

my face and saw only darkness. I thought water hitting me might balance out the clock that seemed to be ticking faster than normal.

The water was the only thing I could feel.

19

I woke up hours later, knowing full well where I was and why I was covered in a mixture of water and sweat. The awe came from the showerhead being turned off. I must've turned it off at some point in my daze and then curled into the fetal position I found myself in later. I couldn't even give myself a short time to ease my mind and pretend I was trying to remember all the events from the night prior. Everything was still fresh in my mind, and I had to use that to my advantage, as opposed to being constantly frightened.

I changed out of my wet clothes, feeling better with something dry against my wrinkly skin. I looked at myself in the mirror after putting on a pair of jeans. My face appeared to be drained of all liquids. Even with the appearance of someone that looked nothing like me, I had to pull it together.

The first person I called was David. The ringing went on too long, but when I was able to leave a message, I didn't hold back.

"David, its Truman. You need to call me back now. Everything went to shit last night and I'm hanging on by a thread. I need you and Goliath to bring the camera. We'll have to meet somewhere new, though. Call me and I'll give you more details."

I hung up, staring at the receiver lying gently in the cradle. I wanted to call Catherine and see if there was any chance she was home. Time didn't seem to be on my side, so I picked up the receiver and spun the numbers that belonged to Goliath. It didn't even make it to the first ring when I heard a knock at the door. The other end of the phone didn't pick up on time, and I put the receiver back in the cradle.

I immediately regretted opening the door. Longhorn and Johns stood with the sun warming their backs. Judging by the crinkled white-collar shirt and dark slacks Johns wore, he was on duty. This time, however, both men had a presence they didn't before. They stood with their backs straight and shoulders square. The bad news didn't hit me until I noticed the smug smile across Johns' face.

"You're under arrest," said Johns.

Longhorn made a sigh like a wife would do when a husband embarrasses her. "Mr. Pierce, we're here because we received a tip you were part of a crime last night." He held out his arms. "We have to take you in."

Johns already had his handcuffs out. He grabbed my right arm and made me spin around so he could get the bracelet around my wrist. I wanted to use my elbow from my left arm to put a beautiful decoration in the middle of his face, but he seemed he was itching for me to make a move. While Johns was close to snapping my arm, Longhorn read me my Miranda rights. Longhorn was nice enough to close the basement door.

Johns paraded me all the way to their unmarked Ford Crown Victoria. It was still early in the morning, but not early enough for some of my neighbors to leave their houses for work. From nurses getting home from the graveyard shift to business men on their way to the next corporate deal, they were all in unison staring at me. The rumors were already starting to spread by the way they held up their phones to get a clear video of me. Johns made sure the spectators had plenty of time to capture the moment.

The Ford was all black with the obvious police antennas sticking out from everywhere. The most memorable thing about the car was the smell. After Johns threw me into the back—right in the middle seat—I could smell the stench of food that must've been sitting underneath their seats and the overuse of car fresheners to make up for it. I felt no prison cell could be worse than the smell burning my nostrils.

The first couple minutes of the ride were spent in silence. Longhorn was driving, using every safety measure he learned as a teenager. Johns would turn his head back to me every few seconds, giving me a smile that said he wasn't dreaming. The first couple of times, I locked eyes with him but then looked out the window, ignoring him. We were about a quarter of the way to the precinct when Johns wanted to start a game with me.

"So," he said, licking his lips, "you thought you were going to fly under the radar from me."

I said nothing.

"I knew you had a hand in Hutchins' death. Your connection with the crime ring was tough to prove, but our witness was the one we were patiently waiting on."

"Stop, Johns," said Longhorn. "Wait until we get to the station, and on tape, before we say anything to the suspect."

"Oh, I'm just having some fun with our new friend." He turned his sights back on me. "I have to say that—"

"How much is Victoria paying the both of you to look the other way?" I asked with a straight face.

This brought everyone in the car back to silence. Longhorn, for the first time, looked at me with bewildered eyes in the rear-view mirror. Johns, doing an *Exorcist* move, spun his whole head at me. The fire in his eyes and the strawberry red across his face were more than any words he could muster. The game just went in a different direction.

Johns said, "What the fuck are you implying?"

"I thought a smart cop like you could fill in the blanks."

"I am no dirty cop!"

"Yeah, that's what every crooked cop says before they are arrested." I smirked. "I got it all from the one you dubbed 'V.' She told me that a number of your brothers and sisters behind the badge are actually working for her. It made sense to me considering the boys in blue act like she is a cat burglar who keeps on slipping through their fingers."

Johns could only breathe loudly through his nose. Longhorn had his eyes more on me than the road. This was more than pinching a nerve.

I continued, "I didn't want to believe it, but since you have done nothing but harass me while the bad guys make a clean getaway, then I think she has a point. The reality is you are either too dumb or you've been in Victoria's pocket this whole time."

And just as I finished the last part, Johns reached both hands to the back, putting his hands around my neck. Longhorn swerved the car all over the road, using his right hand to try and pull Johns back. Johns screamed a mixture of obscenities and false claims. The only thing that hurt was the bad breath coming from his mouth.

Longhorn eventually made it to the side of the road without hitting anyone and pulled Johns away from me. I couldn't make out what Longhorn was saying to Johns over the coughing and breathing I had to catch up on. I took a big gulp of air and used it to laugh. Longhorn told me to shut up.

As Johns huffed and puffed, the real worry came from Longhorn. He looked at Johns, but it was clear his attention was on me. The quiet ones like Longhorn are always the ones to pay extra attention. I could see the pupil looking at me from the corner of his eye. Maybe he wanted to make sure I wouldn't run, or maybe his brain was finally processing the exclusive I'd given.

A few moments went by before Johns stopped whining and cooled down. I thought Longhorn would have to restrain the beast all the way to the station. When Longhorn asked Johns if he had his shit together, Johns nodded. Longhorn did a panoramic turn of his head, checking to see if anyone had been smart enough to film everything that happened. Lucky for the cops, we were on the side of the road with nothing but asphalt and trees surrounding us.

At the station, after they processed me, I was put into an interrogation room. The first hour had me sitting alone. The white walls and gray, tiled floor seemed like I was already in the insane asylum. The only comfort from this was the handcuffs coming off, leaving red marks that wouldn't go away anytime soon. Maybe that was their point for keeping me for so long. I kept controlling my body movement from the two-way mirror that sat to my left. I didn't want to give the crazy guy show they were craving.

The police station was built sometime in the 1950s. The town council had debated many times whether it was worth smashing down and putting up something that would qualify for the twenty-first century. The council figured spending money on a building that was technically still standing wasn't worth taxpayer money. Instead, funds would be used to keep the welcome signs to our perfectly fine, murderous town in pristine condition.

I used the alone time to go over everything I'd prepared to say to them. They laughed at me when I told them I didn't need a lawyer. The smug faces were ready to send me to a gulag, if they could. Longhorn did say something about a witness seeing me last night in the neighborhood. My defense would be this certain eyewitness mistook me for somebody else. I only hoped that the witness hadn't gotten a clear image of me on their phone.

The clock on the wall told me it was about noon when Longhorn entered the interrogation room. He didn't take the metal chair opposite. Instead, he stood by the door, brushing his shoulders off like a dust cloud hit him before entering the room. Longhorn stood with his shoulders back like he had practiced it many times in front of a mirror. Finally deeming himself presentable, he brought his attention to me.

"Ok," he said, "it looks like we're keeping you here overnight."

"Release me."

Longhorn shook his head. "No, our witness won't be back until tomorrow for the lineup. We have enough to hold you for forty-eight hours." He signaled for me to stand. "Let's go."

I stood up, extending my wrists.

"That won't be necessary," he said. He grabbed the triceps in my left arm and gave it a squeeze as a reminder not to do anything.

The basement housed the cozy suites for prisoners. The first thing I noticed when Longhorn pushed me through the door to the holding cells was the drunk taking the first cell to the left. He was completely passed out and didn't look like God herself could wake him. Longhorn told me to keep walking when I gave too much attention to the drunk. There were only a dozen holding cells—six on each side. They looked to be eight-by-eight, with old-fashioned bars you would see in a cheesy western. There were cots that weren't long enough for a child, and, surprisingly, toilets that were still functional. I also noticed rust on some of the cell bars as I walked down. My bedroom for the night was the last holding cell to the right. Longhorn passed me to open the cell door. The only thing that could've made it more comical would be him using giant keys you'd find in a movie to unlock the cell.

"All right," Longhorn said, pointing to the camera above the door, "we'll be keeping an eye on you. I'll be back tomorrow morning." He locked the door while I still had my back turned.

Hours later, a uniformed officer stopped by my cell with a sandwich and canned soda—both looked like they came out of the same vending machine. My stomach growled enough for me to accept both items without complaint. Through the cellophane I could see my dinner was moldy ham. I pretended the sandwich was a New York strip as I ate it and downed the warm soda pretty fast.

Most of my time was spent lying on the cot, keeping my mind jogging while my body wouldn't move. Occasionally, I would look over to see the red dot above the camera staring right at me. I figured I would be like the drunk on the other side of the room and stay asleep.

Or do my best to pretend.

20

Hours later, to my amazement, I was asleep. Even with the metal springs practically piercing my skin, I slept better than any baby. I hadn't slept like that in a long time—well before everything that happened with Danielle. Maybe it was the exhaustion or my acceptance that everything was going to end horribly, but I decided to let my mind go free and to let life carry me for a change.

Normally I don't remember my dreams, but I did remember that night's well because it was a good reminder for my why I was doing all of this to begin with. Not only did I dream of Danielle, but my subconscious went even further back to my first day as a janitor. This was welcome to me compared to picking out every detail of the day Danielle was killed.

Getting the job at the college was easy. I treated my interview with Henderson like I was at a Fortune 500 company. I didn't wear a suit and tie, but I wore a polo and khakis as a way to show the job wasn't beneath me. Henderson didn't even finish his prearranged questions before extending his hand and telling me to show up at six the next morning.

When I did arrive the next day, I hit the ground running with cleaning and other duties. Henderson told me all new people have to start with the bathrooms because that's where everyone at the bottom of the totem pole starts. I figured as much, and then I went out to scrub each toilet in the facility until I could see myself. That was basically my morning.

The afternoon was spent mopping the floors—*a good way to get to know the layout of the college,* as Henderson put it. During this time, all of the students and instructors walked passed me like I didn't belong. They were astonished someone in their twenties could be working as a janitor. The looks were once an embarrassment to me, but over time I learned to pretend they weren't there.

I had just about finished mopping the floors when an overweight student, wearing a T-shirt with a clever quote from Einstein, accidentally spilled his Diet Coke in front of me, getting plenty on my shoes and pants. His face turned into a giant strawberry with three shades of red. He made one apology after another, but I told him it was cool and to move on. I had just put the wet mop on top of the soda when a pair of black high heels that shouldn't have been allowed in the building came into view. I did the classic camera take where I followed the shoes to the tan legs, to the blouse, to the blue top, and then to the blue eyes. She had a smile that made me forget about the soda on me and the floor.

"Hello, I'm Danielle."

"Hey, I'm Truman."

She extended her right hand for me to shake, but I held up my hands to show the mess I had acquired while cleaning. Danielle laughed and put her hand down.

"I hope that doesn't stain your pants," she said, pointing to my feet.

"It's not like they are high quality. I'll live."

She laughed. "Is this your first day?"

"It is. Still trying to figure things out here."

"There's nothing special about this place. You won't have any trouble knowing the ins and outs."

I went to ask her how long she had been working here, but an administrator from behind her called out to her. She gave me one more smile before walking away. It was only a brief encounter, but still one I never forgot. For a place that didn't show me much my first day, it was nice to see one person acknowledge I existed.

My dream flew around for quite a while after that with flashes of other small encounters I'd had with Danielle. We would have more brief conversations for a little over a year until she asked me out. But during those times in-between she had always made me feel like I was actually part of the faculty—more than a janitor. Even before the janitor gig, I had felt pretty low about myself. It only took a smile and friendly conversation to bring me back up.

My eyes opened.

There wasn't any noise or force to wake me, but I knew I had to. It took me a few seconds to remember where I was, but when I did, I could feel a presence near me. I wanted to stay in dreamland for the rest of the night, but I knew what lay beyond the iron bars wouldn't let me. I sighed and lifted myself to a sitting position on the cot. There was a weak light between my cell and the one directly across from me, but the outlines of Victoria and Bald were apparent.

"I must not be dreaming anymore," I said, putting my feet to the floor and the left side of my face towards them.

"You aren't," said Victoria.

Victoria sat in a similar brown leather chair I saw in the Captain's office when I was being booked. Once again, she wore a dark blouse and top like she was treating this as a formal business meeting. Her legs were crossed, showing off her expensive high heels paid for with blood money. She had a neutral look on her face that I wasn't sure should worry me or not.

I did a quick glance towards the exit. The light might've been low, but I still noticed there weren't any guards to watch this go down. Even worse, the red light for the camera was turned off. Victoria made sure the meeting never existed.

I rubbed my eyes. "I'm guessing the boys on your payroll let you in?"

She said, "That's correct. I made sure my men were the only ones running things tonight." She leaned back in the chair. "No one will be bothering us."

"You're all alone, Pierce," said Bald.

Bald did his best at being Victoria's lapdog. He stood behind her, a little to her right. The black leather jacket he wore was the biggest thing the light captured. You could make out some of his facial features from the light, but he made sure to keep a few steps back so I wouldn't forget I was talking with the main boss. He had his arms down, with his right hand holding his left wrist. He kept his shoulders back like he was ready to take a gun out at any second.

I turned my face to Victoria. "And are Longhorn and Johns resting easy up there?"

Neither said a word. I wanted to see if one would slip up and give me the information I wanted. They looked like the type that had played mind games like this before. Fine, if that wouldn't work then it was time to cut to the chase.

"If you're going to kill me, then get it over with already."

"If I wanted you dead," said Victoria, "you would be dead. I would've let you stay dreaming forever, but I'm not going to make it that easy for you."

"So, you want to make my dead body look like a suicide?"

"I could have my guard get his gun out, shoot you, and then we casually walk away like nothing happened." She brushed some hair away from her face. "No, I'm here to make sure you know the plan still hasn't changed."

"And why do you say that?"

"You still owe me one more job."

I sighed. "And you're here to remind me? Do you want to know what happened last night or who did the damage?" I wasn't going to give Vince's name. I'd play dumb and give a bad description of the attacker. First, I had to find Vince.

"I'm well aware of who and what happened."

"He'll be dealt with eventually," Bald said with confidence.

"Just like you dealt with the horse," I replied.

He didn't say anything, nor did his facial expression make any notion that he contemplated my remark. Instead, Victoria made a sweep of her hand against the leather sleeve of his right arm. For a second I thought he might be doing more than protecting her, but I wiped the useless thought away and put my attention back on the boss lady.

"So," I said, "now that you made your point clear to me, what is the next step?"

She said, "Getting you out of here."

"Are you my new attorney?"

"I'm out of the law's grasp, and now you will get a taste of that. Tomorrow morning you will be bailed out."

I snapped my fingers. "Just like that?"

"Just like that. The arrangements for your early release are already being processed."

I made a face that said I was impressed, nodding my head longer than I cared to admit. "And what about this mystery witness?"

"I already took care of that problem," said Bald.

My impressed expression turned to concern. "What did you do?"

"What do you care?"

"I care. What did you do?"

Bald smiled at me, giving the moment a few more seconds so my mind could do flips. "I only talked with the guy. Reminded him what I do, who I work for, and to think about everyone close to him. By the end of our conversation he couldn't remember his own name."

I didn't have any reason not to trust him. Sure, he was an asshole, but he was an asshole that would've given me the truth at any point to see me miserable. They knew even killing strangers would put my mind down a different road. They needed me focused, without emotions. Since I was already in this state of mind, I thought I could try something while they were still looking at me like a caged animal.

"You know," I said, looking straight at Victoria, "everything is only going to get worse before this all ends."

She blinked. "And what makes you say that?"

"Because someone is dead, and everything is far from controlled. You might have your plan ready, but the thing about plans is that they always get broken. Blond didn't expect to be shot in the head that night by some unhinged vigilante."

She pursed her lips. "Where are you getting at?"

"For you to tell me what you know about Danielle. We have already gone past the point of no return. You don't need me as a chauffeur. I told you before: things will only settle down when I find out who killed her."

Her moment of silence was more than enough to know I had gotten into her head. She swayed her heard around like she was in serious thought. The silence had gotten to the point where Bald was about to speak up. Victoria snapped out of her silence like she couldn't believe she'd considered it in the first place.

"No," she said with vigor.

I took my eyes away and hung my head.

"I can take care of my end. You're still going to complete the last task." She moved her hand underneath her chin. "I would also like to remind you not to come up with any bright ideas about running off. If we can't find you, then one of my men won't have trouble finding your spy you sent. Or how about the old bitch that looks like she would welcome death? Do you think that sweet, old granny would even know a gun was pointed between her eyes before it was too late?"

I kept my cool, not letting them see the emotions building. I lifted my head and stared at the bars of my cage like they were people.

Bald tapped Victoria on the shoulder. She got up from her chair. "I have to go now, but in a few hours you'll be free. Someone will pick you up for you final task, just like before, so don't stray far."

And with that, she started to walk away. Bald pushed the leather chair behind her, wheels squeaking.

I lay down again on the cot. I wasn't interested in their dramatic exit. All I could hear were their footsteps and the obnoxious noise coming from the chair. That same sound woke up my drunken neighbor on the other side. He demanded to know what the noise was about. A few seconds went by before he apologized profusely and stopped talking. About ten minutes after they left, the red light above the camera turned on.

I was on the cot with my legs hanging off and the springs digging into my back. Surprisingly, I was able to fall asleep once more, but before I did I tried to figure out this jigsaw puzzle without anyone else being hurt around me. I couldn't see it. I couldn't see how I could make three moves ahead when Victoria had one of her goons with a gun against Thelma's head. I couldn't see how I could get the ace up my sleeve to knock out Victoria without seeing Catherine punched more. I still had David and Goliath, but I could see them

lying dead the second Victoria found out about their involvement.
I couldn't see what winning an unfair game would look like.

The thought of suffering put me to sleep.

21

"Pierce, wake up."

I didn't expect to see sunlight when my eyes opened, but the windows at ground level brought in rays that were able to light the entire room. It felt like I was out drinking all night—head pounding after being on the hamster wheel. My back felt perfectly fine, but my legs needed a minute to wake up. I didn't recognize the voice for a moment as the mouth kept going.

"Wake up, Pierce."

I turned to find Longhorn standing at the cell, arms crossed with the cell key hanging off from one of his hands. He hand on a different cheap suit from yesterday, but it was his body language that said defeat. I knew what he was going to say by the way his scowl was trained on me.

"We're letting you go," he said.

I acted perplexed. "What?"

"I said you're being released now." That time he made his voice louder than it should have been.

"And what about the witness and line-up you told me about?"

Maybe I should've just let him release me without the follow-up question, because he stared at me for a few seconds, probably wondering why I wanted to know. He begrudgingly took the cell key grasped tight in his hand and unlocked the cell door with his head down.

"It looks as if the witness said he was mistaken with the entire thing—something about it being too dark to see anything."

At least Bald was telling the truth about the life status of the witness. Victoria didn't want any more bodies dropping so soon, but words can hit harder than bullets. This was probably why Victoria had stayed quiet for a moment, pondering my request just to tell me what she knew about Danielle.

Longhorn opened the cell door. "Let's get you out of here before Detective Johns makes another scene."

On the way out of the basement, I took one more look at the drunk. He was wide awake, but he sat on his cot like a replica of The Thinker. His fist directly under his chin, deep in thought like he was only a dictionary definition away from total enlightenment. He took a moment to get out of his trance so he could look at me. Instead of unfamiliarity towards me, he shot me a glance of fear. He knew they were here last night to talk to me, and he knew it was about business. It was in that moment I wanted to tell the town drunk I wasn't who he feared. I wanted to grab his head so he would be looking at me directly in my eyes as I stated my case. I wanted him to know by the time I walked out of the room that I was actually on his side, his ally.

Who was I actually trying to convince?

When Longhorn pushed me out of the stairwell and onto the main floor, every cop had their eyes on me. I was ready for Johns to come around a corner and go for my throat again, but he was nowhere to be seen. It was difficult looking at each of the officers and figuring out who was on Victoria's payroll. Each had a look like they wanted to tie an anchor to my legs and push me off a bridge.

It took a few minutes to sign a couple of papers for my release and to get back the few possessions they held. As I put my wallet in my back pocket, I had a clear view of the Captain's office. Through the clear glass windows, Captain Roberts sat in the same leather chair Victoria had occupied only a few hours earlier. He was on the phone, laughing at something. I laughed internally at who was in charge of the town and their claim to the throne. I shook my head.

I told Longhorn I knew my way out of the building, but he wasn't escorting me for my benefit. Johns was standing next to the double glass doors, crossing his arms like a disappointed parent. I wasn't fully awake for any of his drama, so I kept my focus on the door. When I reached out to push the left door open, he jumped in my way. He was still wearing the same clothes as the day prior. Every piece of clothing was wrinkled enough to say he didn't bother to take them off when he slept. Or it could've been his late nights at the police station with the rest of Victoria's bought cops. I kept my eyes on him, even with his coffee breath watering my eyes. Longhorn did his best to keep a hand on Johns' shoulder, but no one could stop the beast.

"Not today," I said to Johns.

"I don't know how you did it, but I'm going to make sure there is enough evidence to put you away forever. You won't ever get an appeal after the horrors I expose about you to the world."

"You love the sound of your voice, don't you?"

He took a half-step towards me, but Longhorn gripped his shoulder. I waited until Johns stepped aside. He murmured something in my direction as I took a step outside, but nothing could faze me at that point.

It didn't occur to me until I was outside that I needed a ride. I figuratively kicked myself for not using the phone while I was being released, but there was no way I was going to walk back in there. My apartment was on the other side of town, so I needed to start walking. I hoped to find a store on the way and use their phone. I didn't want to be out in the open for long but didn't have much of a choice.

Halfway through the parking lot, I heard a faint noise that seemed to grow a little louder. When I recognized my name coming from the sound, I looked to my left and found David running across to catch up with me. He was out of breath by the time he reached me.

"How did you know I was here?" I asked.

He took in a gulp of air. "The murder the other night has been all over the news. When I got your message, I put two and two together. I tried reaching you a number of times, and then started to think something happened. The police records I found last night said you were being detained, so here I am now."

I looked around. "Did you drive here?"

He nodded.

"Good, 'cause we need to get to your place now." We both turned and started for his car. "Call Goliath and have him meet us at your place."

Twenty minutes later the three of us were back at David's. Goliath was already there when we pulled up. Inside, I asked David for a glass of water after I took my place on the right side of the couch. He returned with a brown mug with the face of a German Shepherd on the front. I drank the whole thing in one gulp.

After handing the mug back to David, I started my report with Catherine ending up at my place, bloody. Goliath wanted to grab the camera from his bag, but I stopped him. I told them I hadn't been able to find her since and that they should see if anything comes up for them. They both said, in unison, they would look into finding her.

I then went into the drive out to Blood Springs, where Vince showed up and shot Blond. I didn't leave out any details of the shootout and how Blond was ready to add me to the foundation of dead bodies. The stronger I went into the gory details, the more their faces turned green. And to think they'd volunteered to go with me more than once.

What jolted them was my visitors last night while I was locked up. I told them how Victoria, making her point clear, had the people she paid to let her in and talk to me during the night. I went into how she personally referred to Catherine and Thelma, but she hadn't used their names. That didn't mean she was in the dark about them. They knew the power she had but were still shocked to hear of her reach. All they could do in a situation like that was start the contemplation that I had been doing since last night. We had to come up with something, and fast.

"I need to find out if Detectives Longhorn and Johns are working for Victoria." Before they could interrupt, I continued. "They have been hassling me since the start, and they seem to be on me every step of the way. I want concrete evidence I could use against them."

David said, "We'll look into it."

Goliath remembered the camera and started searching his bag. "Do you want to record now?"

I held up a hand. "Before we do that, the main reason why I am here is that I need to be wired the next time I go. I know, I wasn't sure about it before, but things have changed." I put my concentration on David. "Tell me the miniature video recorder is fixed now."

"Actually," David said, walking into his bedroom, "I think it might be."

It only took him a few seconds, but when he returned his arm was outstretched and palm open. At first glance I didn't see anything, but a second look revealed what looked like a black mole in the center of his palm. I picked up the micro machine, delicately holding it. David wasn't kidding when he said it was Cheerio size. This would be perfect and would never be detected.

"How do I get this on?" I asked.

"Flip it over and there is a clip attached," he said, taking out his cell. "Clip it to your collar so we can do a test run. The video can be broadcast right to my phone."

I did as he said and clipped the device to my collar. Besides it being a different color from my shirt you couldn't tell, or feel, the device hanging there.

I waited a minute while David went through his phone to find the app for the machine. Goliath used the time to get his camera out and power it on. I knew he was ready to record more of my deposition. He checked to see if there was enough battery life and storage for what had to happen next. Goliath knew there couldn't be any problems this time with the recording.

"Ok," said David, "it's ready to go."

When he tapped his phone, a brief zap hit me.

"What was that?" I asked, pulling my collar away from my skin. "A small zap hit my neck."

David's face went into panic. He kept pressing down on his phone like he was giving CPR. He did this for another minute, going through the settings and configuration with the app. He cursed a few times and then tossed his phone on the part of the couch where I'd just sat.

I said, "I'm not a tech wiz like you guys, but I'm guessing the thing is dead."

David huffed, confirming my statement.

"If you order a new one now, would it get here in a day or two?" I asked.

David grabbed his phone back off of the couch, wiping it off like he was apologizing to the machine. I watched as his fingers moved fast to do a quick search. His face went through a number of emotions. It finally settled on hopelessness when he was done scrolling and tapping his fingers.

"It looks like it will take about a week before I can get another one. The standard delivery for the manufacturer seems to be backlogged right now."

There wasn't time to sit around and mope. I took off the micro Cheerio from my collar and sat it on the coffee table. We had to act fast, so my mind raced until the first, non-dumb thought came to me.

"Ok," I said, looking at David, "you need to give me one of your spare phones."

David looked at me. "What?"

"I need to borrow one of your spare phones. I'll hide it in my pocket when they come to pick me up. Without them noticing, I'll call your main number—after you get it programmed into the phone I'll be using—and you can be a witness."

Goliath went to say something, but closed his mouth when he started to ponder. He even held a finger to his lips to make sure he didn't say anything before he thought it out. David, on the other hand, was more optimistic.

"Yeah, that might work," David said. He craned his neck and stared at the coffee table. "I can use a recorder and put the phone close to it so I can record everything. It might be grainy, but it should still be audible."

Goliath shook his head. "No way will that work. Maybe you can get a good enough recording, but," he faced me with determined eyes, "they could easily search you and find the phone."

I gave a shrug. "It's a risk worth taking. There's a strong chance they will find it at some point. It doesn't matter what happens to me. I feel like I'm on borrowed time already, so tricking them with something obvious is more than worth it."

Goliath didn't say anything. His facial expression was the agreement I understood.

David was gone and reappeared just as quickly with an older, rectangular smart phone. He went over everything with me. He showed me the phone's lock screen was already turned off so I could just tap to unlock it. I watched as he programmed his number, giving me a shortcut on the home screen to hit so I could just tap his number. He handed it to me, making a quick remark if I knew how to operate one of these. I may not like technology, but I don't hate it, especially when it could save me. I gave him a look he understood.

"What I want to make sure is when I call you with this phone," I held up the contraption like he never saw it before, "that you pick up and it doesn't go to voicemail."

David held up his hand like he was in court. "I don't care what time of the day or what I'm doing, I promise it will get answered."

I couldn't convince him anymore except for shaking him, so I told him to keep his phone charged at all times. David then remembered to grab the much needed charger for the phone. I wrapped up the cord, and then put both of my new items into my pocket.

We wrapped the rest of our time with Goliath recording the additional story and thoughts over the past couple of days. I didn't shy away from any details I felt would be necessary for the police to use. I also didn't hold back on the corrupt cops that had surrounded the town with innocent smiles. I figured my conversation with Victoria at the police precinct would be enough, hopefully, to make some federal investigators more than interested in the good-natured local cops.

After I got back to my apartment, the first thing I did was plug the charger into an outlet next to my bed and then stuck the other end into the phone. The charging battery icon on the top corner of the phone told me the outlet was working properly.

I then checked in with Thelma. She said there weren't any problems she could think of around the house, but was more concerned with my face, asking why I looked a little beaten up. I told her I slipped and fell, and it was enough for her not to ask any follow-up questions. I would've eaten one of the freezer dinners with her, but I didn't want to be away from my phone for long.

I sat in my apartment, letting the vibes of John Coltrane help me wait patiently. I stared at the basement door for hours. I thought this would be the night where I would be walking out of my place for the last time. The second I heard footsteps, I would rush to get my new phone and get it ready. I wanted that night to be the one where I finally got them.

It wasn't.

22

Four days passed without hearing from anyone. My alertness was still high, but at times, it would take my mentality down. Being juiced up for something twenty-four seven does take a toll. Little by little I stopped staring at the door like a statue and eased up. Hell, I even thought for a moment that Victoria's crew had forgotten about me. Every time I would ease up slightly, my brain would snap me back to what was happening. I kept my phone charged all the time, occasionally checking it to see if David, or someone else, sent me a message.

I didn't just sit around and let them keep me in fear. I used the little time I thought I had to find Vince and Catherine. I mentally had to do a coin toss and went with Vince first. I thought they wouldn't be after Catherine at the moment, but Vince had the biggest bullseye taped to his back.

There weren't many places to check, and I didn't want to ask around mindlessly about a wanted suspect, so I went to the place where I'd first talked to him. When I made it to his place it seemed... different. The place was empty. This was weird since the last time I saw it there were a number of people mourning a death. There were a few cameras I could see as I walked around the house, but they didn't bother me. I knocked on the door a number of times, but only the wind was present. I thought of breaking in, but a place like that would have a number of security systems guarding it. And I didn't need any more police interference. I screamed out Vince's name before I drove away.

After trying his palace, I decided to see if maybe Catherine would be hiding at her place. She still came across as mysterious, but she had let me know while at my place where she lived. The garden condo she owned was only a few miles from where she worked. She was on the first of three levels. When I pulled up, her place was just as dark and empty as Vince's. I knew knocking on the door would be futile, but I did it anyway. I knocked and knocked until an elderly neighbor came out and asked me why I was making so much ruckus. Disappointed, I got back in my car and went home.

That night I waited around, pacing for something to happen. It didn't take long for them to call on me the first two times, so I knew they would be here shortly. I only had an apple for dinner— my stomach wouldn't let me hold down a lot of solids. I was dressed in jeans, a long-sleeve shirt, and a jacket that could perfectly hold the phone. There were zippers on the outer pockets of the jacket to store my phone without anyone noticing. I don't think I even took off my clothes for those days.

Around midnight, still wired awake, I heard a car slow down in front of my place. The engine sounded different from the Charger, but that didn't mean someone else would be grabbing me for a ride along. Normally, my neighborhood was the place where everyone was asleep by this time, and I didn't believe in coincidences.

When I heard the engine cut off I went for the phone next to my bed. I took it off the charger and held it in my hand like a newborn. I heard footsteps getting closer to my apartment as my thumb hovered over David's number. I was just about to dial when I heard a voice I didn't expect coming from the other side of the door.

"Truman, are you there?" said Catherine. Her voice sounded a little different, but it still belonged to her.

The surprise almost made me drop the phone. I put the phone back on the charger and tucked it away next to the bed. She knocked a few more times before I answered.

When I opened the door, I saw someone battling with many forces. Catherine, this time, stood straight in the doorway. The first thing I noticed were the bruises and cuts surrounding her face. Sure, the blood was wiped away, but those scars and bruises would be with her for a long time, if not the rest of her life. The right side of her face was bloated with purple and green skin, while the other side had some skin hanging off. She made no attempt to put makeup over her fresh scars. It was a good reminder for me to get back at all of them.

"Come in, come in," I said.

She quickly walked inside. I took a few steps outside to do a panoramic view—woods to street. Nothing in sight told me anyone was watching, but that didn't give me the peace of mind I was hoping to receive.

After I was back in and closed the door, I quickly pulled one of the kitchen chairs for Catherine to sit. Sitting opposite of her, we didn't speak for the first few moments. I wanted her to feel like she could relax, and she looked as if her mind was settling down to communicate. Her left hand was cupped over her right hand, easing her nerves. She finally looked at me, giving me the all clear.

"Dumb question," I said, "but are you ok?"

"I'm as ok as I can be."

"I've been looking for you for the past couple of days. I went to your place and you weren't there."

She looked down like she was embarrassed. "I have been hiding out with different friends. I didn't want to go back to my place because I had the image of either the blond thug or someone else beating me up again. I've been going to a different house every night so that I wouldn't be followed." She brushed a piece of hair away from her face. "I thought about calling you a number of times, but I didn't want to risk it."

I calmly nodded. "I understand, but you don't have to worry about Blond anymore."

"Why?" Her eyes were asking me what I had done.

I didn't realize until then that she had been off the grid the entire time. Maybe I thought she would've heard it somewhere, but her face said differently. I gave her a smile to change the fearful mood in the room.

I said, "Because that piece of shit is dead."

She had trouble finding her words. "Did you, I mean, what hap—"

"He's gone and won't be hurting you again."

"Was it you?"

I shook my head. "It was Vince—Danielle's brother."

I went over everything that had happened the night I last saw her. When I got to the part about how Blond provoked me into fighting him, she tensed up. It wasn't until I told her how Vince crashed our party, by running over Blond and putting a bullet in his head, that she returned the smile to me. She felt the same odd satisfaction as I had.

"I can't say I'm disappointed he's gone," she said.

"No, I doubt anyone will be." I wiped my forehead. "So, how did you manage to be undetected by Ramone and Blond the night they came for me?"

"It wasn't easy. When I was in the bathroom, I heard the door open, but the voices were low and I couldn't tell who it was. After what happened to me, I didn't want to walk out and say hi to your guests. Luckily, all three of you had your backs turned, giving me just enough time to run under your bed and wait for you guys to leave." She took a deep breath. "When I did hear that asshole talking from the bathroom, I wanted to go in there and rip his throat out. I just kept my hand over my mouth so none of you could hear me cry."

All I could do was nod my head. "How long before you left my place?"

"Only a few minutes. I wanted to make sure no one ran back into your place out of curiosity. I went straight to a friend's place when I was certain the coast was clear."

"And what did you tell your friends when they saw you?"

"That some guy beat me up—I wasn't lying. I just didn't go into any of the details. It's easier to say a guy beat you up because they won't ask any personal follow-up questions." She looked at me and smiled. "No, I didn't say you were the guy or anything. I just made up a random name—Andrew or Chris or something—and went with that."

She then went on about how scared she was—and still is. I felt more like a therapist, listening as she unloaded what felt like a lifetime's worth of inner dwellings. At times she cried and I would hand her a napkin. Other times she would laugh out of nowhere, probably realizing she was getting overly emotionally and wanted to lighten the mood. Didn't matter, because I was happy she was alive and speaking her mind to me. When she finally got out everything she built up to say, she made a serious face you would during a job interview.

"Ok," she said, "what's next? Do you have any idea what's going to happen?"

"I still have one more job to do. I might not make it out, so I already made sure David and Goliath take the recordings of me and give them to the authorities."

Catherine's face turned perplexed. "David and Goliath? As in my students?"

"Yeah. They have been helping me this entire time. I made sure they recorded my every step of the way through this shit journey. They know if something happens to me, they'll send it to people they can trust. If so, they'll upload it all over the internet."

"That's a smart idea." Her legs crossed, and she leaned forward like she wished she had come up with that idea. "What do you want me to do?"

"Nothing for now."

"Nothing?"

"What I want is for you to go back home and rest that bruised face of yours."

Her face turned concerned. "And what if they're waiting for me at my place?"

"They won't be. They're only after me right now. I don't think they know about David or Goliath—just you. The guys know about you, as well. If they believe something might happen to you, they'll contact you. What you need to do is wait until my time with Victoria is done. I'll let you know if there is anything more after Victoria's errand run."

She nodded. "I understand."

I took a moment to collect my next thought. "I know the past few days haven't exactly been easy on you, but did you find anything new about Danielle, her killer, or Victoria's operation?"

"I didn't. There wasn't much time for me to do any research or detective work."

"Yeah, I figured that I would ask anyway."

The hour was late, not realizing we'd spent a lot of time going over everything we had to tell. There was even some time at the end where we were looking at each other to make sure everything that had to be said was said. I asked her if she wanted to crash at my place again, but she told me she was more than eager to get back to her place and feel her bed again.

When she left I decided to take my own advice and crash. I hit the bed, staring at the ceiling for a few seconds until I realized I forgot to tell Catherine about my new device I acquired from David. I could've given the number to her just in case an emergency happened with her again, but I ended up thinking I wasn't going to have the gadget for long.

Before I had any chance of going over what my plan was or what it felt like to see Catherine alive again, I passed out.

23

It got to the point where I couldn't ignore other responsibilities in my life.

The next morning, after drinking a third cup of coffee at six in the morning, Henderson called me and told me to come into work or I would be fired. The "I can't because drug dealers need me as their chauffer," excuse wouldn't cut it. He was losing his patience with me and I lost all my excuses. His voice was one I hadn't heard in a long time: a parent confronting their rebellious teenager.

Before work, after getting dressed, I figured taking the phone would be more necessary than keeping it away from me. I had kept it charged all night. I put the phone into my pocket and then made sure I had all the secondary items I needed for the day.

I made sure to get to work extra early to ease any tension Henderson had towards me. That still didn't work. He commanded me to mop up the piss all over the boys' bathroom floor. That morning pretty much had me doing similar work, with Henderson giving me all kinds of grief. I figured he would get tired early in the afternoon or he would just cool down.

And I ended up being right about the former.

Most of the afternoon Henderson had his head on his desk, sleeping away. Halfway through my lunch break I had to step outside the janitor's room from the loud snoring. Even after lunchtime was up for the both of us, he kept going like it was a marathon. No way would I wake him up so he could resume his negative attitude towards me.

It was about an hour before I had to leave for the day when Mr. Sleep decided to wake up and return to his job. He woke up like someone had shaken him. He flailed his arms and spun his head in a cartoonish way. When he took the minute finally to come back to earth, he looked at me like he was bewildered I was in the same room. I was ready for more rowdiness from him.

"I need to take a leak," he announced.

"Don't let me stop you."

He stumbled out of the office, walking away from the closest men's bathroom, but I wasn't going to enlighten him. The longer he was gone, the better it would be with the remaining minutes of the day.

Ten minutes passed with no sign of Henderson. I wasn't worried about him as he was the type of person to be gone for a while and then show up later like nothing had happened. If you tried to help him, then this would remind him of his age and he would get offended. I kept to myself at my desk.

During those ten minutes I slipped the phone out of my pocket and put it in the top drawer of my desk. Having the mechanical brick in my pocket annoyed me. The thought of getting off soon had me excited enough to change out of my janitor's uniform and back into my street clothes. I was going over some recent orders management had given to me and Henderson when I heard the door open behind me.

"That took you long en—"

I turned and saw Bald standing in the doorway. He wore the same black leather jacket I assumed he was born in. His eyes were dark, holding their sights on me.

"You couldn't wait until I got off work?" I said.

"Time to go."

I looked behind him. "Just you today?"

He didn't look away. "Just me. Let's go."

I tried again to get Bald to look behind him, but he wouldn't budge. The phone was tucked away in the top drawer and no way of getting it out without him noticing. The way he looked at me like every guard would with a prisoner on the way to the electric chair was enough for me to know I needed the device. I stood up, giving up any chance of getting the phone, when Henderson barked behind Bald.

"Watch out, sonny," said Henderson. "You're blocking my way!"

Bald turned to Henderson, giving me the few seconds I needed to get the phone out of the top drawer and back into my pocket. When Bald turned back to me, annoyed, I was still sitting in my chair.

"Now," said Henderson, "you don't look like a student. What are you doing here?"

Bald didn't answer. Instead, he turned to me and his hand went under his jacket where his .45 ached to be used.

I quickly got up and put an arm around Bald, smiling. "This is my cousin. He's in town for the week and I was going to show him around. He was supposed to pick me up after I got off my shift, but he's here a little early. That's why I was eager to leave today."

Henderson huffed. "Your cousin could've waited outside." He pushed past me and Bald so he could sit down again at his desk.

Bald still didn't say a word during the exchange. I had to get both of us out before Bald became impatient and sent Henderson to an early grave. I gave Bald a look that told him I would take care of it. Bald stayed at the entry of the door while I stood next to Henderson. The Old Man had his head buried in recent repair orders.

I said, "So, since my cousin is here, and it's about time for me to leave, would it be ok if I left now?"

If there was any time in his life where Henderson didn't have to act like an old tool, that was it. Death was standing only a few feet away from us, and all Henderson could pay attention to were the work orders. I couldn't even give him a warning with my eyes without catchingBald's attention.

Henderson grumbled. "Yeah, fine, you can leave early. Just make sure you are here, on time, tomorrow."

I breathed a sigh of relief.

I practically pushed Bald out of the office. Never have I had the urge to leave that building in such a hurry. There were people eyeing Bald and I, but no one started any small talk with us. I kept my speed normal and had my head down so everyone would get the picture of a person who only wanted to leave. Bald seemed just as eager to get out of there as me. He kept the same pace with me all the way out of the building.

Bald led the way as I looked around for the Charger in the parking lot. Instead of the car I had driven two times before, we reached a Nissan Sentra I wouldn't have expected. More surprising, Bald reached for the driver's side door. He still kept his mouth shut, and I wasn't going to argue, so I got into the passenger's side. As Bald started the car, I glanced his way, waiting for some kind of explanation.

"Any chance of you telling me what this is about?" I asked.

He stayed silent as he drove the car onto the main road.

It didn't occur to me at the time when I put the phone in my pocket, but in the car, I was thankful the machine was in my front-right side pants pocket. Had I been driving, I wouldn't have attempted the next steps.

Not even a few miles down the road, I nonchalantly put my hand into my pocket. I kept my face pointed towards the passenger-side window so I didn't give him any hint of what I was trying to do. Luckily, during those days I wasn't needed for Victoria's chores, I had played with the phone enough so I knew exactly where on the home screen my contact list was and where to press David's number. My jeans were dark enough when I hit the screen that the machine lit up without Bald noticing. There wasn't a passcode on the lock screen, so I used my thinking to go about the next steps. I hit the area where the contacts were and then tapped it once more to quick dial his number. I never did check the volume level on the phone, so I quietly held my breath. A few seconds went by without the bells and whistles, making me exhale slowly.

We passed the same cemetery Danielle where was buried. The cemetery was on our left, making both of us do a quick look. Bald didn't show any signs of sorrow—for Danielle or anyone else buried there. I lowered my head for a quick prayer. I prayed for Danielle's soul and for everything to have been different. Bald saw me and snorted.

"I never understood why you made all this noise for that bitch," he said. "She wasn't even that hot."

Under normal circumstances my fist would've already gone across his face, but I had to remind myself what was in my pocket and what the endgame was supposed to be for him and the others involved. Getting into a fight with Bald would certainly have the same outcome as Blond.

At a traffic intersection, Bald put the brakes on at a red light. This was when I second guessed myself about whether or not the call went through. I needed to know that David was on the other end, listening and recording everything. An all-white Ford Crown

Victoria sat next to us at the light, waiting to take a left. I used this as an opportunity to distract Bald.

"Have those cops been tailing us?" I asked, motioning towards the car.

Bald slightly turned his head enough for me to take out the bottom of my phone to get a sneak peek. As I feared, the call didn't go through. I went to start the process all over again when, from the corner of my eye, Bald started to turn his head back to me. I used my thumb to quickly push the phone back in my pocket.

He said, "If that eighty-year-old grandmother is a cop, then I'm an FBI agent."

"Don't let appearances fool you."

The light turned green and the car was back in motion.

Once again, my finger was in my pocket, fidgeting around the phone to get it to do what it's supposed to do. Part of me couldn't believe how annoying these things were and why people would even bother with them in the first place. I kept my cool, tapping in the place I knew my contacts were, and then tapping, once again, for the single contact stored away. I had to sit and pray David would actually pick up this time.

I kept my senses on high alert. If the call reached David, then the last thing I needed was dead silence for the car ride. Both times I went with them, no one had told me much, but I needed some clue as to where I was going so David could send the cops if things went south. I cleared my throat, lifting my leg slightly so the receiver could hear us better.

"Are you going to tell me where we're going?" I asked.

He remained silent.

I sighed. "Look, I've already been on two of these errand runs. I haven't run to the cops, nor have I done anything to ruin Victoria's plans. I've only done what I have been told to do, and all I'm asking now is where we're going."

His voice was low, but his tone made up for it. "No. Stop talking."

"If you're going to kill me, then just get it over with now. Driving me all over town just so you can put a bullet in my head is a waste. Why would you keep a secret like where you're taking me? Does Victoria have some rule that dead men shouldn't know where their resting place will be?"

Instead of taking out his .45, he exhaled like he was being deflated. "The old factory that shut down a while back—on the river." He gave me a look that was as sharp as a knife. "Now stop talking. Your voice annoys me."

After another fifteen minutes of driving, we ended up exactly where he told me. The factory he referred to was an old tire plant that went out of business over ten years prior. The brick building from the 1930s was a beacon of hope for blue collar workers in the area, but eventually crumbled from the greed of the people running it. The building was by a river where there weren't any residents within miles. It shouldn't have come as a shock that a building with weeds growing on the side and half the windows broken by kids would be the spot for criminals to gather.

The first thing I noticed was Ramone's Charger parked right next to Bald's ride. The Charger looked brand new. In the short time since I saw the vehicle, all the damage was wiped away like it went through a car wash. Not even a dent was visible. I looked around to see if there were any other cars in the area, but saw nothing.

When we got out of the car, I went to take a sneak peek at the phone, but Bald kept me on my toes.

"Stay in front of me." He pointed to a rusted metal door at the front. "Head through there."

I did as he said and proceeded to the front door, thinking how perfect of an opportunity it would be for him to take out his gun and end things now. There was no point in running for it. I didn't have enough time to reach the river without a number of bullets going through me. The only way I could possibly win the fight against Bald was for him to play it dumb and stick the gun in my back, giving me enough space to spin and wrestle the weapon from him. But he played it smart and kept a distance of more than five feet away from me the whole time.

No shots to the back happened when we reached the rusted door. I tried to take a peek through the window, but the dirt and grime were worse than the actual ground. It didn't matter what was in the building. Everything seemed like it was thought out—through and through. The only possible saving grace was hopefully listening on the other end of the phone. I could hear Bald breathing hard behind me.

"All right," he said, "open the door slowly and go through."

24

The inside of the old factory wasn't as bad as I thought it would be, but it still looked like a place that closed its doors a long time ago. The leftover machinery and conveyer belts had dust and spider webs covering all over the place like you would see in a haunted house. There was a second level surrounding the sides, but the middle of the room had a cathedral ceiling. There were some tires and boxes piled in the back of the main floor. The big revelation to me was the roof had few holes in it, leading a little leakage in and rusting the inside like the exterior.

"Around the corner on the right and up the stairs," said Bald.

I stopped taking in the scenery and started walking.

The stairs were closer than I had expected when I made the turn around the corner. The metal staircase had more dust on it than the actual gray coloring. Walking up, I saw footsteps and fingerprints on the rails that had pushed away the dust recently. There were at least two different types of footprints, but I couldn't just stand around and examine it like I wanted.

At the top of the stairs was a hallway with rooms on both sides. The rooms to the right of the hallway had windows so the bosses could keep their sights on the little people downstairs. I didn't recognize the downstairs, but the power was flowing through this building. The hanging lights in the hallway were powered on and looked like they had fresh bulbs. It didn't amaze me what door Bald wanted me to go through.

"The third door on the left," he said.

It was safe to say Ramone would be behind the door, but the quick flashes of different scenarios entered my head. The first, and most obvious, thought was Ramone pulling the trigger just as I entered. Another was multiple people in there, happily shooting at me over and over again. Many more like that popped into my mind, but it didn't matter. The point to it all was my way of trying to fight my way through, but that was a long shot.

Bald told me once more to open the door.

I opened the door.

The first thing that hit my senses wasn't a bullet, but Vince tied up. Sitting in a metal chair, Vince sat with rope tied across his chest, arms, and feet. He had duct tape over his mouth. His back faced the far wall, a few feet away. He sat in the center of the room with a hanging light hovering over him like you would see in an interrogation scene of a cop movie. His head was down; blood from the hits he'd taken dripped down onto his shirt and pants.

I was so engulfed by the sight of Vince that I didn't see Ramone standing only a few feet away from him. When I did look over at Ramone, he was in the middle of wiping the blood from his hands with what once was a white towel. He looked up at us like we were right on time.

"Come in," said Ramone. He motioned to Bald to close the door.

Bald went to push me, but I took the steps needed for him to miss. I heard him shut the door as I stared at Vince. I couldn't even help him stop the bleeding. I tried to take another step toward him, but Bald told me to stay still.

Vince, lifting his head and opening his eyes, caught sight of me.

Whatever little strength he had left was hit with a mental adrenaline shot. His eyes opened wide and he started to scream muffled noises through the duct tape. He rocked the metal chair back and forth like he was going to charge me, but Ramone smacked him with an open hand across his face.

"And I thought he was angry with me," said Ramone, smiling.

Vince stopped moving. Even with the blood dripping into his eyes, he couldn't stop with the hound-dog stare at me. His face was red, not just from the blood but also the realization his path looked to be at the end, and I was going to be in the same room to witness it. He wanted me dead and he knew he wasn't going to see that before he left the earth.

I said, "Vince, I—"

"Shut up," said Bald.

"I want you to kn—"

Ramone took out a nine millimeter Beretta from his back waistband. "Talk to him again and I'll shoot you." He held the gun on me for a few seconds before lowering it.

Vince had messed up dearly, but this wasn't the way I wanted to see him go. My search for him would've ended with me turning him over to the cops—alive and breathing. I also wanted him to know I wasn't part of the operation. It would've taken him a long time to process that, but he would eventually understand. Vince and I had taken two different paths to find the truth, but they led to the same place: we would enter the afterlife together. My Sherlock Holmes approach against his scorched earth strategy didn't get us what we needed. Even with multiple paths, there didn't seem like there was one that could make it out alive with the answers we needed.

I focused on Ramone. "So, what now? I was brought along, again, to see how tough you want me to think you are?"

Ramone eased his way behind Vince. He took his gun and put it against Vince's head. Vince closed his eyes and wept. Everyone in the room knew Vince was seconds away from his brains ending up on my shirt and jeans.

Ramone said, "Victoria wanted to make sure you knew what it meant to hurt our business. She saw this as an opportunity to squash as much resistance towards her as she could."

From behind, I could hear Bald take the .45 out from under his coat. I didn't turn my head but could sense he had the gun trained on me. Ramone was still going with the speech he had probably been practicing for days, but I was already tired of everything.

I said, "You brought me all this way to kill me? Stop being a pussy and do it already."

Ramone laughed. "No. What I was going to say is—"

Right then, the door behind me and Bald opened. After the wind hit us, we looked up to see Victoria standing in the doorway. She wore a dark trench coat that went slightly past her knees, and it awed me that no one heard her matching high heels clicking down the hallway. Her right hand drummed on the doorway, evaluating the situation with a panoramic movement of her head. She nodded as she walked in without closing the door.

"I... you said you weren't going to be here," Ramone said.

Bald was equally bewildered, staring at Victoria while keeping the barrel of the gun pointed at me. I guess they wanted me to be shocked, but I wanted to laugh at how out of their element each one acted.

Victoria didn't even acknowledge my existence. She nonchalantly moved out of the frame of the door. Her gaze on Vince told me her main purpose for being there. She looked at him like she was meeting him for the first time, but at the same time knew about his existence her entire life. He was the worm and she was the hawk. She focused on Vince while speaking to Ramone.

"I had a change of heart and wanted to see this for myself," she said, gently touching the left side of Vince's face. "He really made a mess of things, and I couldn't just sit back and imagine what would happen."

Vince turned to me. His face went from vengeful to sorrowful. The running tears made the dried blood wet again. He started speaking to me once again, but his muffled words were ones I could tell came from a place of respect, not animosity.

Victoria cupped underneath his chin and turned his face so his eyes wouldn't leave her again. "I just want you to know that stupid bitch you called a sister got what she deserved."

Vince didn't react in any way, finally accepting his fate. His blue eyes seemed to go lighter. All the muscles in his face calmed so much it looked like his skin was hanging off. He aged twenty years within a few seconds.

Victoria took out a six-inch blade she carried in her trenchcoat pocket. She gently put the blade through Vince's Adam's apple. His eyes widened while the breathing from his nose intensified. Victoria savored the moment, staring at his expression like she wanted the memory forever. She retracted the blade from his throat just as gradually and delicately as she put it in. Blood oozed out of the hole from his neck as Victoria stood straight with her shoulders back.

The only thing I could do was watch Vince die. I wanted to figure out a way to take the gun away from Bald, but when I looked from the corner of my eye, he had his gun trained at my head. One move and I was dead. I could hear Vince choking on his own blood, gasping for air.

Victoria walked over to me, finally acknowledging my existence. She held up the bloody knife, but instead of sticking me in the throat, she wiped the blade on my shoulder. When she was satisfied enough with the cleanliness, she moved the blade in front of my throat.

"And you thought I wouldn't notice your stealth move, didn't you?" she said.

"I didn't know where Vince was or—"

Victoria laughed. "No, that bug was easy to find and squash."

I looked at Vince as he turned white. He couldn't stop coughing, and blood trickled from his nose. He didn't have the strength to keep his head up, dropping his chin against his chest.

She continued, "I'm talking about the small team you wanted to keep hidden." Her face turned to the door. "Bring him in!"

With a force that landed him on the floor, Goliath was shoved into the room. My heart stopped. He was facedown on the ground, duct tape binding his wrists. The left side of his face was covered in blood from a wound originating from his head. He coughed a number of times, trying to catch his breath.

Another one of Victoria's cronies walked through the door. He was vastly taller than anyone else in the room. From his jet black hair and toned physique it wasn't a surprise to me why Victoria had picked him. He didn't carry a gun, but his MMA fighter body said he didn't need one. He picked up Goliath by the back of his shirt and got him to his feet like he weighed less than a feather. Victoria pointed to the opposite side of the room from me, and the bodyguard pushed Goliath there violently. He stood behind Goliath with a bear grip on the little guy's shoulder.

Goliath blinked a few times. When his eyes adjusted to the light in the room and he caught sight of me, his jaw gently dropped. I gave him a nod so he could keep his cool and not make things worse. The idea that he was here and David wasn't disturbed me. I wanted to figure out a way to communicate with Goliath on the whereabouts of David, but Goliath seemed like he was busy trying to keep his bodily fluids from spilling out.

"I didn't get the name of your colleague, Mr. Pierce," said Victoria. "I just made his acquaintance only a short time ago. Luckily for all of us he was heading in the same direction as everybody else." She walked over to him and cupped her hand under his chin and squeezed. "You thought we wouldn't notice, did ya?"

I said, "Let him go."

That made Victoria turn and face me. "We both know that isn't going to happen. My plan was to kill you at the same time as Mr. Hutchins."

I glanced over at Vince. He didn't look like he was moving at all. A smaller stream of blood was coming out of his neck. If he wasn't being taken away by Death now, then the Grim Reaper was waiting for his turn.

"But," continued Victoria, "I would rather let you live. I want you to know how you can never outthink me. I'll kill your little friend. Make you watch him bleed as you did with Mr. Hutchins. I'll put enough fear in you that you will look behind your shoulder every two seconds for the rest of your life."

I needed to buy more time. Victoria lightly swung her blade around like it was a Samurai sword. She semi-turned to Goliath, smiling at him like a guard would before flipping the switch on a death-row inmate. I had only seconds to act, blurting out the first thing I knew would give Goliath some more time.

I said, "And what about the information you said you would give me about Danielle?"

This halted Victoria. She stopped smiling, turning to me like I told her she forgot her purse. She lowered the blade down to her side. Her face scrunched up a little, thinking of what she would say to me as opposed to the carnage she was already inflicting. She got close enough to my face I could feel the hot breath from her mouth hit me.

"That bitch thought she was God. I wanted to recruit her because she had the connection to the college I was looking for." Victoria motioned to Vince's body. "Having him buy up a good amount of my supply made me think his sister would be more useful than just another customer. I approached her, but she was resistant. The last time we talked she gave me this whole speech about not wanting to join and that she would rather be dead than turn out worse than her brother." Victoria smiled like she had the punchline ready. "It looks like she got her wish. So, I gave her one of my cards as she was leaving and that was that."

As Victoria walked over to Vince, I looked at Goliath. Fear smacked across him, but I tried to eye him so we could figure out some way to communicate with each other. He was just about to look at me when Victoria turned back to me, making me dart my eyes back at her. Victoria stood next to Vince, grabbing his hair and lifting his head up.

"Who would've thought this entitled, coked-out rich boy would live longer than his sister." She dropped his head, the meatball smacking against his chest. "Danielle was someone who could help me get more of the younger crowd than what I already have. Business hasn't exactly been good for me lately, so I wanted to find new ways and fresh faces. People like Danielle are beautiful and can attract the younger, dumber crowd into buying whatever."

I lowered my face, thinking how everything finally made sense to me. Yes, this wasn't the news I expected, but it did shed light on what I needed. Victoria misinterpreted this as melancholy when she studied my face.

"Aww, you thought she was the damsel in distress you wanted to avenge. I can tell you that miss perfect had nothing to do with my operation." She put her hand on my shoulder. "Thanks for the free errand runs you did for me, by the way."

Goliath knew his time had come. Victoria put her gaze back on him, reminding herself what she had to do next. I once again tried to distract Victoria's attention with another question, but she wasn't having any more stalling. Goliath tried to squirm, but he couldn't get more than an inch of wiggle room from his human force field.

Just as Victoria took another step towards Goliath, Longhorn and Johns burst into the room with their guns drawn. Bald, being the closest to the door, was knocked in the face by Johns when he wasn't fast enough to aim his gun. Bald laid at my feet, knocked out. Ramone put his gun against my head, using me as a shield. The monster behind Goliath tried to crouch his massive body behind the lanky individual to use as a shield, too.

Longhorn and Johns surveyed the room. Longhorn had a gun pointed at the man holding Goliath, and Johns looked like he was trying to aim at Ramone, but his gun was angled more towards me. Both men side-eyed Victoria, who hadn't made a step since they joined the party. Did she know her world was crashing down or that the reinforcements arrived on time? Longhorn and Johns were more curious about the knife she hadn't dropped.

This was where the worlds collided with each other. I still didn't know who to trust, nor did I think the actual rescue had shown up yet. I kept my mouth shut for once, watching as all the faces were trying to make sense of the situation. It felt like I was playing Russian roulette with five out of the six chambers filled with bullets.

I only had a few seconds before everything descended further into hell, but I still had to use my time wisely. Luckily, this time Goliath was already looking at me when my eyes darted towards him. I gave him a glance down, and he was smart enough to notice my left hand against my leg. My plan would only work if we were on the same wavelength. I folded my pinky and thumb, leaving the three other fingers pointed downward.

My ring finger folded behind my hand.

I gave him a nod and he returned it back.

My middle finger folded behind my hand.

We locked eyes. Both of our faces dripped sweat.

My index finger disappeared.

With one swoop, Goliath lifted his right foot and brought down everything he had on the bodyguard's foot. The man arched down in pain, opening space for Goliath to lean forward and bring his entire head into the man's face. They both went down, blood gushing out of the thug's nose.

Ramone pointed his gun at Goliath, and the second before he pulled the trigger, I put my hand under his elbow and lifted. The shot went into the ceiling as I tackled Ramone to the ground. We wrestled for the gun, each trying to point the weapon at the other opponent. The weapon flew out of his hands and against the wall. I punched Ramone across the face, smashing his head against the floor and then moving on top of him. He tried to throw a couple of fists at me, but they were easy to block. My emotions were on fire, and I was going to take out my anger on that sorry, worthless shit. Fist after fist pummeled his face. I didn't want to stop until I was out of energy, and it felt like I had enough to go for years. Blood and skin flew off his face.

While I was knocking the shit out of Ramone, a couple of shots were fired. There was screaming and yelling coming from all different echoes of the room. Whatever happened didn't faze me in the slightest. No one bothered to interfere in my business with fists or bullets.

It got to the point where I stopped and looked down at my bloody fists and then to the bloody face that wouldn't be healing anytime soon. There were a couple of teeth next to Ramone's head from when he spat them out. His eyes were shut and his body not moving. I didn't have any more fists to throw.

I stood up, examining what had happened while I was occupied. Bald had woken up at some point and thought it would be a great idea to charge the cops. Three bullets to the chest made sure he would never get up again. Goliath lay on the floor, but with no bullets in him. He looked around for a few seconds to make sure no one was still firing. The hulking monster cowered in the corner. Blood from his nose and piss from his pants were coming out simultaneously. Victoria, on the other hand, hadn't moved an inch when the bullets and fists were flying. She kept her place in the middle and just let the mayhem ensue.

When I faced the cops, Johns looked at me, not like I should be thankful they showed but that he was still angry with me. His head was tilted forward a little, but his eyes were only on me. His face, even after shooting someone, still carried resentment like everything wasn't done. His breathing was heavy, his chest rising up and down. I went to break the tension.

I said, "How did y—"

He pointed his gun at me and fired.

That moment lasted less than a second in real time, but stretched out for an eternity in mine. The bullet came straight at me, going so slowly that I could physically see it, but too fast for me to get out of the way. This piece of metal that I thought was going to end between my eyes flew past my head. It was less than an inch from my dome, a bee whizzing by my ear.

Back in real time, I swung around after the realization that the bullet wasn't meant for me. When I turned I saw Ramone with a bullet hole where his nose once was. He was back on the ground, but this time the walls were coated with his blood and brains.

Even Longhorn didn't know what happened until a few seconds after. He'd had his back turned when Johns fired, so he also spun like he heard a bomb go off. His eyelids looked like they were being held open by spirits. He examined everything before realizing the scene was secured, his face relaxing. He probably thought his partner actually put a bullet in me.

I looked back at Johns. He smirked as he holstered his pistol. He walked out of the room, leaving his partner to clean up the aftermath.

25

A few hours later, I sat with Goliath on an old-style police bench back at the cop shop. The police had already questioned us, but they told us to stick around a little longer before they could release us. The police station had turned into a madhouse. We watched hundreds of people going in and out like it was a train station. This town was already feeling the repercussions of the events from earlier.

Vince was dead. The paramedics rushed to get to the factory, but the man was dead before they made it into the building. I watched from outside with law enforcement as they carried his body out in a body bag. I was even curious if that was the same body bag they used to carry out Danielle from the school. One way or another, both siblings were now joined together again in the afterlife.

The paramedics examined me and Goliath. They didn't see any problems with me, but they thought it might be a good idea for Goliath to go to the hospital to have his head looked at. He said his head looked worse than it felt. When the paramedics tried to persuade him once more to go to the hospital, Goliath, in an assertive tone, told them to get lost. A near-death experience can toughen anyone.

Back at the factory, Goliath told me David was fine—at least, when he last saw him. That was confirmed by Longhorn, who told us he had spoken to David when we got to the station. Longhorn told David we were doing well now and that he could stop by the station to pick us up when they were done questioning us.

While we waited, Goliath filled me in on how he ended up in the same room with everyone else. When I called the second time, David answered. He could hear everything perfectly that was happening to me in the car and that I clearly needed help. While he listened in, he called Goliath, telling him to get over to his place as fast as he could but to wait outside and keep the engine running. David was tired of sitting back, and by the way things were going with me in the car, he wanted to distract Victoria's crew as long as possible before the cavalry could show up.

After picking up David, Goliath was instructed to go to the factory where David heard Bald telling me we were going. David brought a second phone—his personal cell—and used that to call Longhorn and Johns. I don't know why David called them after I told them about my hesitance with the police duo, but my guess was David panicked and called the two lead detectives he had been hearing about over and over.

David was still on the phone with Longhorn when they pulled up at a distance to the factory. They saw me for a brief second with Bald before we went into the building. Goliath wanted to get a closer look, so he got out of the car and started towards the factory. Unaware that Victoria would show up, Goliath was attacked by her henchman from behind without warning. He tried to run, but the monster picked him up and threw Goliath against a tree, injuring the side of his face. Goliath, remembering he left the keys in his car, didn't want David to be caught as well, so when the beast lifted him, Goliath yelled for David to drive away.

I also caught Goliath up with everything that happened to me.

I used this as a way to pass the time we had before they could let us go. I kept reassuring him that things would be better now. I was half-telling the truth because I saw the finish line approaching, but we still needed a few more steps to cross before giving the all-clear signal. All I could say was Victoria was being interrogated, her top two men were dead, and her lapdog was sitting in a jail cell with piss-soaked pants. What I didn't mention was the number of people that were employed by Victoria that were still roaming free. Sure, we cut off the snake's head, but the body was still slithering.

While I mentioned all of this to him, a number of uniformed cops came through the front entrance, wearing badges that didn't belong to the precinct. They all went into the back for a while. They reappeared and started arresting cops right before our eyes. The looks on those officers I had seen around town for so long was just as much of a shock for them as it was for us. The out-of-town officers and suits didn't waste any time rounding up people and either sending them downstairs into the cells or cuffing and taking them out front for the world to see. At least five officers, just from what we could see, were taken away.

Longhorn walked out from the back. My first thought was the confounded appearance of him not wearing handcuffs and being taken away to the basement cells. He was able to cover up most of the splattered blood on his white button-down shirt, but there were still a few spots. He sat next to me on the bench when he caught sight of us. Longhorn seemed like a week's worth of sleep wouldn't get him back to normal. From his pockets, Longhorn handed back each of our phones.

"Both of you will be released shortly," he said.

I motioned towards the basement cells. "It looks like you finally got the crooked cops in your precinct."

"The ring leader is still in the interrogation room, singing like a song bird. She's giving up as many people as she can so she doesn't see the inside of a prison. Even if she can give up everyone that worked for her, it will still be difficult to wipe away the murder charge."

"How much time do you think she'll get?" asked Goliath.

Longhorn shrugged. "Depends on what the D.A. can put together and offer her. The digital videos and information we got from your friend won't help her."

"I guess this is a perfect time to apologize for accusing you of being bought by Victoria."

"It wouldn't hurt," he said. "The day you accused us, it hit me like lightning. There had been an investigation going on for some time about potential corrupt officers. Your accusation only furthered my search into an Internal Affairs investigation into my precinct. We had our suspects but didn't have the proof until now."

"And Johns was never a suspect?"

Longhorn shook his head. "He was never a suspect. The man has his rough edges, but he never went outside the law for extra cash."

I smirked. "And is Johns ready to throw all this in my face?"

"He figured since you aren't a bloodthirsty killer, and you don't believe he is an assassin-for-hire cop, then he thinks you two are square."

The three of us sat there for a quiet couple of minutes, watching as the chaos continue without breaking. No one talked to us, but they were doing sprints for the phones and radios. People were bumping into each other, talking over one another about how all this could've happened in the first place. I figured this place hadn't seen this much action in a long time. It looked like they had their work cut out for them through next year.

"Listen," said Longhorn, "I don't think anyone would mind if you two wanted to leave now. Do you have a ride?"

I said, "Yeah, a friend of ours should be here shortly."

Longhorn pointed to a dark brown door in the side of the building. "That is an exit. You might want to think about using that one because the TV stations are parked in the front."

"Thanks, Detective."

Just then David pushed his way through the front door. The lights and voices from the outside poured over David as he caught his breath. An officer tried to stop David from getting past the front desk, but Longhorn waved him through. David looked at us like we were Christmas morning. We gave him a hug as he told us how relieved he was that we made it out alive. Goliath gave me a look that said he had enough and wanted to get as far away as possible. The three of us started for the side door, leaving Longhorn on the bench.

"And Pierce," said Longhorn.

I turned and looked at Longhorn as he started to get up.

"We don't want to see you around anymore," he said, smiling.

I returned the smile. Longhorn went back to helping the other officers interrogating Victoria. I wanted to tell him that I never want to see the inside of a police station ever again, but bit my tongue.

As the guys exited, I turned around once more and saw Johns coming out from the back. I was about to turn and leave, but he saw me at the exit. We each stood in our spots. Finally, he nodded to me, and I returned the gesture. For the first time he wasn't out to get me, and his face remained neutral—the closest to a smile I figured I would ever get from him.

Outside, there weren't any reporters to greet us, but we could hear the circus happening around the corner. David told us he couldn't park near the building, so he parked in the opposite direction from the cameras and lights. He told us it was near—a quarter of a mile down the street.

The cool nighttime air made it easier for me to walk and think. The three of us didn't say a word on the way to the car, and I was grateful to use that time to plan my last move. Most of the silent time I had at the precinct was figuring out how I would arrogantly confront the killer before the cops. There was a moment when I wanted to tell Longhorn about someone they could pick up now for Danielle's murder, but between the anarchy at the station and my own desire for closure, I kept my mouth shut. I needed my end to this bloody journey before the law could get their hands wrapped around it.

When we got into the car, I sat in the backseat while Goliath took the passenger's side. I heard Goliath give an exhale like he was safe. David adjusted the rearview mirror until I saw his eyes glaring right back at me.

"I'm just happy it's over," David said.

"There's still one more thing we need to do," I replied.

They both turned their heads towards me. David was stupe-fied by my statement, but Goliath looked at me like he had an idea of what I was going to say next.

"And what do we have to do now?" asked David.

I inhaled a deep breath. "I'm going to need you to pay for express delivery."

26

Everything led to this point.

I sat in a dark room in a dark leather chair watching the dark nighttime sky through the slits in a window curtain. I was in the killer's place, waiting for the perpetrator to get back. Luckily, this person didn't have a security system, so breaking in through the window was easier than anticipated. I didn't touch anything else, and the things I had touched I wiped away with the handkerchief in my coat pocket. Breaking in was something I thought I would never do, but I had done a bunch of firsts since Danielle's murder.

I waited around for a little over an hour. I wasn't hungry, thirsty, or uncomfortable in any sense. During my quiet time I pictured Danielle and all those lost along the way. Finding Danielle in her own classroom, seeing her brother being killed in a similar way, the bullet ripping through Blond's head. That these were tragedies no one should ever see only bubbled the anger within me.

But my emotions couldn't stop me from forgetting the plan and keeping my head clear. I had to bury whatever I wanted to do to this person and think about what needed to be said and done. If I let my anger get the best of me, then mistakes would certainly be made.

The police had not been around to confront the individual, giving me the necessary time I needed to say what I had to. It had been only a day since Victoria was captured, but she was still giving names away. There were a number of cruisers all over town during the day, doing several cleanups at once. David or Goliath would call to give me updates earlier in the day to see if anything had changed. I only wanted this time, and then I could wash my hands of the whole ordeal.

My mind snapped out of it when I heard the key turn the lock. The door opened and the owner walked in without seeing me. The darkness covered me well. There was whistling coming from the person, and the sound of keys being tossed on the small wooden table next to the door.

Catherine turned on the light switch and the room illuminated. The light made a clear picture of her face. It looked like her wounds were healing but getting worse at the same time. Her back hit against the wall, and she made a squealing noise when she caught a glimpse of me.

"Jesus, Truman!" she yelled. "You almost gave me a heart attack. I thought you were another one of Victoria's strong arms."

There wasn't any point stalling. "You need to answer for your crime, Catherine."

Her face went from stunned to curious. "What are you talking about?"

"The fact you killed your 'friend.' The same person I have gone through hell with, but blind to the fact the killer was in front of me the entire time."

Cautiously, she started to move away from me. The kitchen to her left was a few feet from her. She kept her hands out like I would be busy looking at those as opposed to her feet. She moved like I didn't notice her inching towards the other room.

"Stay where you are," I said, standing up from the chair.

She did as I told her.

Catherine became a statue when I stood up. Her face didn't show any sign of being nervous, nor did she make any attempt to scream for help. It looked like her mind was at work, writing up the defense.

"I'm guessing you're wearing a wire," she said, crossing her arms. "That would explain the time you spent with the cops yesterday."

I lifted the black, long-sleeve shirt I wore and spun around calmly once to show nothing attached to me. After I lowered my shirt, I emptied the pockets in my jeans, pulling out the white fabric to show nothing but lint in them. She seemed a little more satisfied as I pushed my pockets back in.

"I didn't say anything to the cops about you. Not yet, at least. I came here, by myself, to ask you why you did it." I paced back and forth, keeping some distance between us. "I should've picked it up right away. It felt strange that Ramone already knew about me before I knew him. I chalked this up to Vince tipping him off, but you did come into the picture at the same time. But it wasn't just that one time, seeing as they were pretty much on top of me every time. I forgot the lesson on keeping your friends close and your enemies closer."

"And that makes me a murderer? Coincidence?" She wasn't denying anything yet.

"Being a part of Victoria's drug empire doesn't make you a murderer. Not until she mentioned something that pointed me to you. She wanted to expand with Danielle—meaning she already had connections at the college." I put my hands on my hips. "Victoria told me she had deep connections all throughout town, but it's not like she went through every name with me."

Catherine shook her head. "You're still not making your point."

This was where I had to turn up the heat. Going on coincidences wasn't doing anything to her. I needed to catch her, and that meant twisting some things around.

I said, "You already know about Victoria being caught?"

She nodded.

"Well, she's giving up everyone, and my guess is she's about to give you up—or just did."

Catherine shrugged. "They'll get me on some drug charges. That's different from murder."

"Except how I told Victoria what you did after putting the pieces together."

Catherine stopped smiling or showing any signs of confidence.

I continued, "She told me how Danielle fit into everything. It took me only a few seconds to piece everything together. I then told Victoria what I knew, and it took her the same amount of time to put the puzzle together. Let's just say that all this anarchy over the past couple of weeks because of you set Victoria on a rampage. She didn't believe someone from her crew would be stupid enough to kill without her knowing, but she couldn't think of a better explanation. She didn't think you would be on the run yet, but she saved the best for last—you."

Catherine shook a little. She did her best to keep it all in.

"The sad part is Danielle didn't want anything to do with that lifestyle. She turned down Victoria's offer."

She stopped shaking and threw on a smile that could make the blind cringe. "Danielle absolutely wanted that life."

"And did she actually say anything to you?" I crossed my arms. "The day you killed her, you confronted Danielle in her classroom. She probably told you she wasn't helping Victoria, but the sight of the card Victoria had given to Danielle set you off. You were consumed with jealousy because you wrongly thought the beautiful and popular teacher was going to become some superstar in the same business you wanted to climb the ladder in."

Catherine's body eased with the realization she couldn't out-run me anymore. Her shoulders slumped a little and the muscles in her face relaxed. "Not bad detective work."

"What did you end up doing with the murder weapon?"

"I cleaned the blood off the pen I had with me at that moment and threw it in one of the trash bins before exiting the school. Chances are good that you or that old man threw it out."

All I could do was nod my head and internally exhale. I uncrossed my arms, moving my right hand to my waist. I took off the Cheerio camera attached to the bottom front of my shirt. I held up the device, turning it back between me and Catherine.

And to think David debated whether or not to pay extra for overnight delivery.

Catherine's face turned white. She understood completely as the situation became clear for her. She knew it was over. Her eyes followed the small machine I held between my thumb and index finger. She didn't bother to ask what it was, nor did I have to explain.

"Hope you got all of that, David," I said, holding the machine in front of my face.

I took the Cheerio and put it in my pocket. At first, I thought she was going to attack me. She stood between me and the exit. Her stance begged me to hit her, to get all the frustration out of my system. Her legs were spread a few inches and her knees bent slightly. She extended her arms and touched her wrists together.

"Go ahead and arrest me with your invisible handcuffs," she sneered.

I pointed to the dark brown sofa. "Sit down."

She strolled over with a smile on her face. When she sat, she put her back against the backside of the sofa and crossed her legs.

There was a light brown coffee table in between me and her. In one swoop, I put my left hand under the table and flipped it a few feet to the side, crashing the unlit candle and three magazines unto the floor. I stood before her, a foot separating us. I looked down on her the same way God would look down on her in the reckoning. She didn't change her face when I started to speak up.

"If the cops weren't on their way, they are now."

She didn't respond and she didn't have to. We both were waiting on what I was going to do next. I was stalling, acting more like a rent-a-cop waiting for the actual law enforcement to show up.

Catherine met my eyes. "Do it already, pussy."

My fists balled up just as red as my face. The steam coming out of my ears made Catherine's lips turn into a maniacal smile. I had gone through hell to find the devil, and all she could do was look at me like the whole situation was a joke.

I started to raise my right fist, when an image made me stop. Instead of Catherine in front of me, I saw Danielle's face. We were back at Fitzgerald's piano bar, listening to the pianist and saxophonist play a melody. This had nothing to do with death or crime or following leads or looking for clues. It was about two people who enjoyed each other's company. It was the realization that it wasn't just a thought that a woman actually was interested in dating a janitor. It was Danielle telling me she enjoyed listening to jazz and asking my recommendations on other artists to listen to. It was about two people who found a connection.

The police sirens in the distance snapped me back. I started for the door. I couldn't look at Catherine anymore. Enough blood had been spilled. As I approached the door, Catherine gave one more quip.

"I would do it all over again, Truman."

"I know you would." I didn't look back at her, and my guess was she didn't look at me.

When I opened the door, I took both my hands and put them on either side of the frame to hold myself up. My head felt like an anvil, but I kept my sights forward. I listened the entire time for Catherine, but all I could hear was the soft movement on the sofa. She made no attempt to flee or talk anymore shit.

The lights were weak at first, but grew brighter through the oak and pine trees. I drowned out the noise with my own self-satisfaction to the thought that I could actually go home knowing everything was done. A couple of Catherine's neighbors either looked out the window or stepped out of their units when they heard the sirens. The mechanical patrols stopped within twenty feet of where I stood.

The red and blue lights enveloped me.

Acknowledgments

I would like to begin with my gratefulness towards Apprentice House Press and the staff who worked hard to make my dream come true. Thank you for taking a chance with a first-time novelist and helping me every step of the way.

I would also like to thank my family for being there and their continued support. Mom, Dad, Will and my sister-in-law Hayley for being there whenever I needed them the most and cheering me along all the way. To my cousin Abby for being patient with me as I overshared the book and process with her.

My friends who gave me support during the long journey I went on. Special thanks to Christine who cheered me on all the way to the finish line. Thank you to everyone who stood by me through the entire process.

And lastly, but certainly not least, thank you to my editor, Melanie. Your wisdom and support were the foundation I needed to go through the hours upon hours of work needed to reach my full potential with the novel. Thank you for teaching me what constructive criticism means.

About the Author

Born and raised in Maryland, Patrick Simpson received his M.A. in English and Creative Writing from Southern New Hampshire University. Through years of trial and error, he found his passion within crime fiction. His work has appeared in publications like Mystery Tribune and The Penmen Review. He currently resides in Montgomery County, Maryland. He is a member of the Maryland Writers' Association. *Pierce* is his first novel.

Apprentice House Press
Loyola University Maryland

Apprentice House is the country's only campus-based, student-staffed book publishing company. Directed by professors and industry professionals, it is a nonprofit activity of the Communication Department at Loyola University Maryland.

Using state-of-the-art technology and an experiential learning model of education, Apprentice House publishes books in untraditional ways. This dual responsibility as publishers and educators creates an unprecedented collaborative environment among faculty and students, while teaching tomorrow's editors, designers, and marketers.

Eclectic and provocative, Apprentice House titles intend to entertain as well as spark dialogue on a variety of topics. Financial contributions to sustain the press's work are welcomed. Contributions are tax deductible to the fullest extent allowed by the IRS.

To learn more about Apprentice House books or to obtain submission guidelines, please visit www.apprenticehouse.com.

Apprentice House Press
Communication Department
Loyola University Maryland
4501 N. Charles Street
Baltimore, MD 21210
Ph: 410-617-5265
info@apprenticehouse.com • www.apprenticehouse.com

Printed in the USA
CPSIA information can be obtained
at www.ICGtesting.com
LVHW021354021123
762345LV00009B/67

9 781627 204941